FAVORITE
FABLES
— AND —
FAIRY
TALES

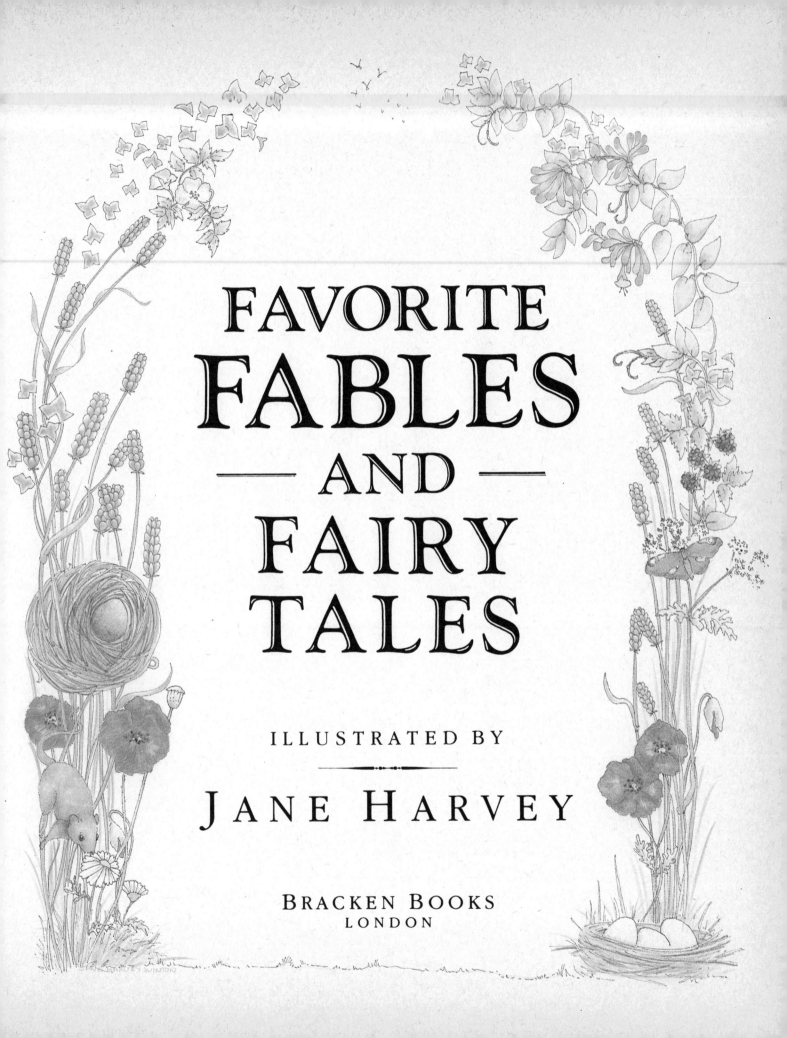

FAVORITE FABLES AND FAIRY TALES

ILLUSTRATED BY

JANE HARVEY

BRACKEN BOOKS
LONDON

This book was first published in 1988 by Bracken Books
a division of Bestseller Publications Ltd
Princess House, 50 Eastcastle Street
London W1N 7AP, England

World Copyright, Text & Illustrations © Bracken Books, 1988

ISBN 1 85170 197 4

Printed and bound Hungary

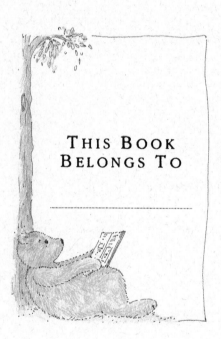

THIS BOOK
BELONGS TO

....

Contents

Contents

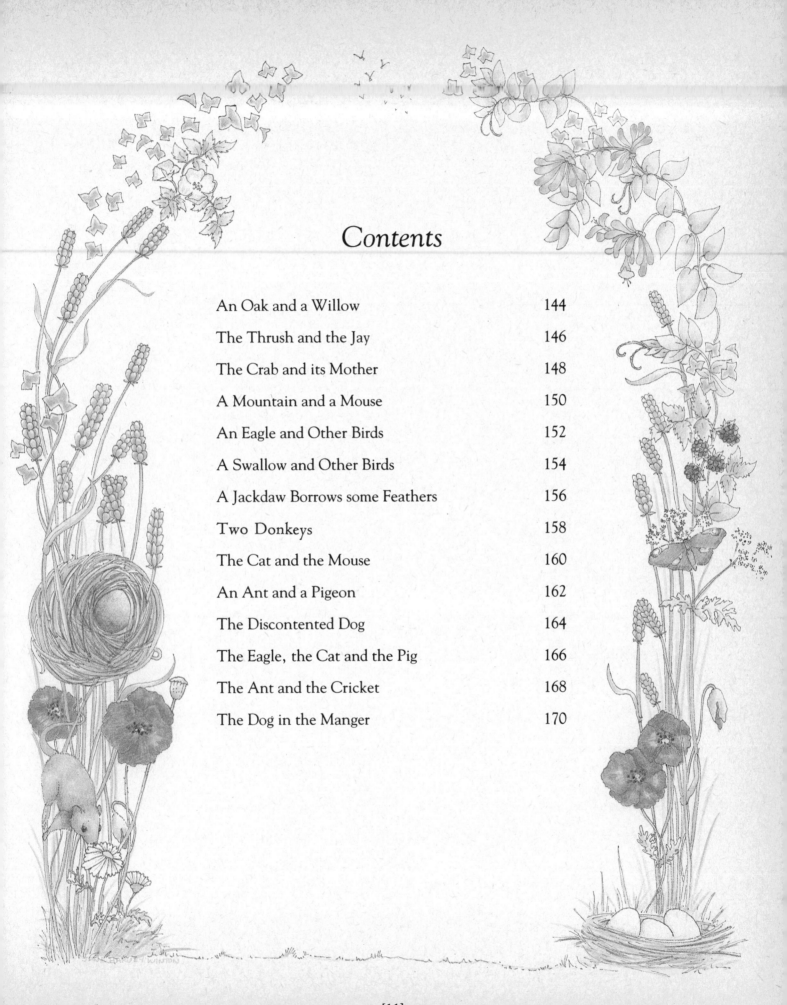

Contents

Goldilocks and the Three Bears

Once upon a time there were three bears who lived in a house right in the middle of a wood. The first was a Little Tiny Baby Bear, the second was a Medium-sized Mummy Bear, and the third was a Great Big Daddy Bear. Each bear had his own porridge bowl; a small bowl for Little Tiny Bear, a standard bowl for Medium-sized Bear, and a large bowl for Great Big Bear. And each of them had a chair; a small chair for Little Tiny Bear, an ordinary chair for Medium-sized Bear

and a large chair for Great Big
Bear.

One breakfast time after
cooking porridge the bears
found that it was much too
hot. They decided to go
for a walk in the wood
while the porridge was
cooling down. As
they were playing in
the woods, a little
girl happened to
pass by their

house. She was called Goldilocks and she was a most inquisitive child. There in front of her stood the bears' house and she just could not resist going right up to it and taking a quick peep in through the window. The first things that caught her eye were the three bowls of porridge, piping hot. They looked delicious! Goldilocks suddenly felt very, very hungry. She tiptoed round the front of the house and poked her head around the door to see if anyone was at home. Nobody was there. So she marched right into the house and the smell of steaming porridge made her feel hungrier than ever. She picked up Great Big Bear's spoon and tasted his porridge. *Ouch!* It was far too hot. So she tried Medium-sized Bear's porridge. *Ugh!* It was far too salty. Then she tried Little Tiny Bear's porridge and that was neither too hot, nor too salty. It was just right. And so Goldilocks sat down at the table and ate it all up, every single drop.

After breakfast, as Goldilocks felt rather tired, she decided to have a rest. She sat down in Great, Big Bear's chair. It was too hard. Next she tried Medium-sized Bear's chair. It was too soft. And then she sat down in Little Tiny Bear's chair. That was just right. But the porridge must have made Goldilocks too heavy for she suddenly heard a nasty cracking sound

and before she knew where she was, Goldilocks was sitting on the floor and the chair was all in pieces.

After that Goldilocks decided to explore upstairs. There in a bedroom she saw three beds, a Great Big bed, a Medium-sized bed, and a Small Tiny bed. She lay down on the Great Big bed – but that was too hard. Then she tried the Medium-sized bed, but that was too soft. So finally she tried the Tiny Little bed and that was just right. In fact it was so comfortable that Goldilocks fell fast asleep.

Just about that time the three bears decided to return home to eat their breakfast. The first thing that Great Big Bear saw was a spoon in the middle of his porridge so he called out: *"Who's been eating my porridge"* in his very loud voice. Then Medium-sized Bear saw that her porridge had been spilt and she called out: *"Who's been eating my porridge?"* Then the Little Tiny Bear looked at his bowl and all he could see was a spoon in the middle of it, with no porridge in the bowl at all so he cried: *"Who's eaten my porridge?"* and he started to cry.

Then Great Big Bear looked at his chair and saw it was all messed up so he growled: *"Who's been sitting in my chair?"* And Medium-sized Bear cried: *"Who's been sitting in my chair?"* And last of

all Little Tiny Bear looked at his chair and sobbed: *"Who's been sitting in my chair and broken it all into pieces?"*

Then the Three Bears marched up the stairs to see if they could find the culprit.

As soon as Great Big Bear looked at his bed he bellowed: *"Who's been sleeping in my bed?"* in his deep, gravelly voice.

And when Medium-Sized Bear looked at her bed she cried out: *"Who's been sleeping in my bed?"*

And Little Tiny Bear stopped crying just long enough to point to his bed: *"Who's that sleeping in my bed?"* he sniffed in his squeaky little voice.

The cries and commotion that followed woke up Goldilocks and the sight of the Three Bears standing close to her bed gave her such a fright. Without a second's hesitation she leapt out of bed and jumped straight out of the bears'

bedroom window. She might well have injured herself, for the ground she landed on was extremely hard. But Goldilocks did not stop, not even to look at her grazed hands and knees. She ran and ran and ran all the way home without turning around once to see if the Three Bears were following her. You will be glad to learn that Goldilocks arrived home safely and the Three Bears never saw her again.

The Twelve Dancing Princesses

Once upon a time there was a king who had twelve beautiful daughters. They slept in twelve beds in a single room. The king was jealous of his daughters and each night the door to their room was shut and bolted, but each morning the shoes by the princesses' beds were quite worn out. Nobody could discover why. The king declared that if any man discovered the secret of the worn-out shoes he could choose whichever princess he wanted for his wife. But whoever failed after three days would be put to death.

A king's son took up the challenge. In the evening of his arrival he was taken to the chamber next to the princesses, to keep watch. Soon he fell asleep and in the morning he found the princesses' shoes full of holes. The same thing happened the second night and again the third night. And so the king ordered the prince's head to be cut off. Other princes came but the same thing happened to all of them.

Now, by chance, an old soldier was travelling through a wood near the king's palace when he met an old woman who asked where he was going. "I do not really know," said the soldier, "but I want to discover where the princesses dance."

"Well," said the old dame, "that is no very hard task. Just don't drink any of the

wine which the princesses will give you and pretend
to fall asleep."

The old woman then gave him a cloak, saying:
"As soon as you put on that cloak you will become
invisible."

Shortly afterwards the soldier offered his services
to the king and when evening came he was led to
the outer chamber. Just as he was about to lie down,
the eldest of the princesses brought him a cup of
wine. Secretly, he threw the wine away, then
lay down on his bed and began to snore
loudly. At once all the princesses got out of
bed and dressed in front of
the mirror. As they were

dressing the youngest said: "I don't know why it is; you are all so happy, yet I feel uneasy."

"You simpleton," said the eldest, "you are always afraid. Have you forgotten how many kings' sons we have tricked? As for this soldier, even without our sleeping potion he would have slept soundly."

The eldest princess then clapped her hands. Instantly a trap door flew open and her bed dropped into the floor. The soldier watched as they stepped down one after another. The soldier jumped up, put on the old woman's cloak and followed them. In the middle of the secret stairway he accidentally trod on the gown of the youngest princess, whereupon she cried out: "Help! Someone is tugging at my gown."

"You silly creature!" scolded the eldest, "it is nothing but a nail in the wall."

At the bottom of the stairs they found themselves at the entrance to a most delightful grove of trees whose leaves were of glittering silver. The soldier broke off a little branch – *snap*: "I am sure all is not right," wailed the youngest, "did you not hear that noise?"

"It is only the sound of the fairy princes shouting for joy at our approach," countered the eldest.

They came to a second grove of trees whose leaves were of gold and to a third whose leaves were of glittering diamonds. From a tree in each grove the soldier broke off a branch.

Finally they reached a great lake where twelve little boats waited with twelve handsome princes in them.

Into each boat stepped one of the sisters. The soldier joined the youngest princess and her prince and as they rowed across the lake the prince remarked: "I do not know why it is, but though I am rowing with all my might the boat feels heavy and I am quite tired."

On the other side of the lake the boats landed. In front of them stood a fine castle. Inside the castle each prince danced with his princess until dawn when their shoes were quite worn out. Then the princes rowed back over the lake and there took their leave. When the tired princesses approached the secret stairway, the soldier ran on before them and lay down on his bed.

In the morning the soldier said nothing about his discovery, but resolved to see more. He followed the princesses on the second night, and on the third night. When the time came the soldier was taken before the king who asked where his twelve daughters danced at night. The soldier answered: "With twelve princes in a castle under ground." And he showed the king the three branches.

The princesses confessed everything and the king asked which of his daughters the soldier would choose for his wife. "I am not very young, so I will have the eldest," he replied.

They were married that very day, and thus the soldier became heir to a great kingdom.

Hansel and Gretel

Once upon a time there was a woodcutter who lived with his wife and two children at the edge of the forest. He had little in the world he could call his own and he was so poor that he had scarcely enough bread for his family to eat. At night he lay on his bed, restless and full of care.

"What is to become of us?" he asked his wife. "What shall we do?"

"Listen to me," she replied. "Take the two children out early tomorrow morning and give each of them a piece of bread. Then lead them right into the middle of the wood, where it is thickest. Build up a fire for them, and go away and leave them alone, for we can no longer keep them here."

"No, wife," said the husband, "I cannot leave my children to the wild beasts of the forest. They would soon tear the poor things to pieces."

"Oh! What a fool you are!" answered the wife. "In that case we must all starve together." And she

nagged him and nagged him
until he agreed at last to
carry out her plan.
Meanwhile the children,
lying awake in bed,
overheard everything that
their father and stepmother had said. "Now we are
abandoned," thought Gretel, and she began to weep. But
Hansel crept to her bedside, and said: "Do not be afraid,
Gretel, I will find an answer."
He got out of bed and went outside into the cold night. The
moon shone brightly on the white pebbles in the little
courtyard in front of the cottage. Hansel put as many
pebbles as he could into his pocket, and returned to the
house. Soon he fell fast asleep.
Early in the morning, before the sun had risen, the
woodman's wife came and woke them up: "Get up
children," she said, "we have to go into the wood. I
have a piece of bread for you but take care of it and
keep some for the afternoon."
After they had walked for a while, Hansel stood still
and looked back towards their home and a little
later he turned to look again, and then again,
until his father said: "Hansel, why do you keep
turning and lagging behind so?"
"I am stopping to look at my white cat that
sits on the roof and wants to say good-bye
to me," answered Hansel.

"You little fool," said his stepmother, "that is not your cat; it is the morning sun shining on the chimney-top." Now Hansel was really staying behind to drop one white pebble after another along the road. When they came to the middle of the wood their father said: "Run about children, gather up some wood and I will make a fire to keep us warm." So they piled up a little heap of brushwood, and set it on fire and as the flames burnt bright their stepmother said: "Now, settle by the fire, and go to sleep while we cut wood in the forest. Be sure to wait there till we come and fetch you."

Hansel and Gretel sat by the fireside until late afternoon. They believed their father was still in the wood, because they thought they could hear the blows of his axe. But the noise was that of a bough which he had hung on a tree, and as the wind

blew it backwards and forwards against the other boughs it sounded like the strokes of an axe.

When it was quite dark and no one came to fetch them, Gretel began to cry but Hansel said: "Wait, Gretel, till the moon rises." And when the moon rose he took her by the hand, and showed her the pebbles along the ground glittering like new pieces of money and marking out the way.

Towards morning they arrived at the woodman's house, and he was glad in his heart when he saw them again,

for he hated leaving
them alone. His wife also
seemed to be glad, but inwardly she
was angry and burned with rage.
Not long afterwards when they were
again almost without bread Hansel and
Gretel heard their stepmother say to her
husband: "The children found their way
back once but now there is only half a loaf of
bread left for them in the house. Tomorrow
you must take them deeper into the wood and
lose them completely, or we shall all starve."
The woodman did not dare to disagree with
his selfish wife. When the children heard their
plan, Hansel decided to gather up pebbles
again, but that night when he tried to open
the door he found his stepmother had locked
and bolted it. But he comforted Gretel, and
said: "Sleep in peace, dear Gretel! God is very
kind, and will help us."
Early in the morning a piece of bread was
given to each of the children, and while they
were walking through the woods Hansel
crumbled his piece in his pocket and
scattered crumbs on the ground.
"Why do you lag behind, Hansel?" asked
the woodman, "be on your way."
"I am looking at my little dove, sitting
upon the roof, who wants to say
good-bye to me," replied Hansel.
"You silly boy!" said the wife, "that is
not your little dove; it is the morning
sun that shines on the chimney-top."
But Hansel still went on crumbling
his bread, and throwing it on
the ground. And thus
they advanced

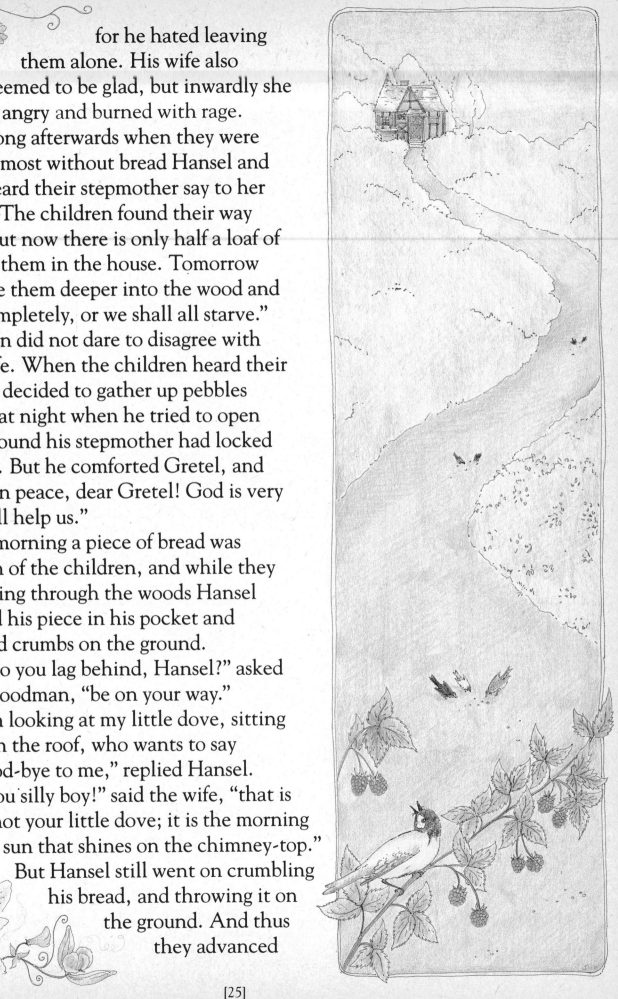

further and further into the wood, to a part they had never seen before in all their lives.

The woodman and his wife built a large fire and said they would come in the evening and take them home. The children waited and waited but no one came. "Wait till the moon rises," said Hansel, "I shall then be able to see the bread which I scattered and it will show us the way home." At last the moon rose, but when Hansel looked for the crumbs they were gone, for hundreds of little birds in the wood had found them and picked them up. The children were soon lost in the dark wilderness. All night long and all the next day they wandered about, till at last they lay down and fell asleep.

The next afternoon, when they were fainting with hunger, they came to a strange little hut. It was made of bread, with a roof of cake, and windows of candy sticks. "Now, at last, we can sit down and eat till we have had enough," said Hansel. "I will eat the roof and you, Gretel, can eat the windows."
But while Gretel was picking at the candy sticks, a shrill voice from within:

"Nibble, nibble, little mouse, Who's nibbling my house?" The children answered: "The wind, the wind, That blows through the air."

Next, Gretel broke out a pane of the window, and Hansel tore off a large piece of cake from the room, but just as they were starting to eat the door opened and a wizened old lady hobbled out. Hansel and Gretel were so frightened that they let fall what they had in their hands. But the old lady nodded to them, and said, "Dear children, where have you been wandering? Come inside with me and you shall have something good."

So she took them both by the hand and led them into her little hut, and brought out plenty to eat, milk and sugared pancakes, apples, and nuts. Then two beautiful little beds were got ready, and Gretel and Hansel laid themselves down, and thought they were in heaven.

But in fact the old lady was a spiteful witch who used her pretty candy house as a trap for children. Early in the morning, before they were awake, she snatched up

Hansel and shut him up in a pen in the stable. The witch next shook Gretel, calling out: "Get up, you lazy little thing, fetch some water and go into the kitchen and cook something good to eat. Your brother is shut up all ready for fattening, and when he is fat enough I shall eat him." So the best food was cooked for poor Hansel while Gretel got nothing but crab-shells. Every morning the old witch hobbled out to the stable and cried: "Hansel, put out your finger, that I may feel if you are getting fat." But Hansel always stretched out a bone, and the old woman, whose eyes were dim, couldn't see it, and thinking always it was Hansel's finger, wondered why he fattened so slowly.

After six months of this she finally lost patience. "Gretel," she squawked at the girl, "quick, get some water. Hansel may be fat or thin but I shall kill him tomorrow and cook him." "First of all we'll bake," the witch cackled. "I've heated the oven already and kneaded the dough."
"Creep in," said the witch

as she pushed Gretel towards
the oven, "and see if it's properly heated, so that
we can bake the bread." Gretel hesitated: "I don't know how
I'm to do it. How do I get in?"
"You silly goose!" retorted the witch, "that opening is big
enough. See, I could get in myself." She crawled towards the
oven and poked her head into its dark opening.
At once Gretel gave her a tremendous shove and pushed her
right in. She then slammed shut the door, and drew the iron bolt. How the
witch yelled, it was quite horrible; but Gretel did not stay. She ran straight to
Hansel, opened the stable door, and cried: "Hansel, we are free, the old witch
is dead." How they rejoiced and jumped for joy! And as they no longer had
cause for fear, they entered the old hag's house. There they found boxes and
caskets stuffed with all kinds of pearls and precious stones. "These are even
better than pebbles," said Hansel, and crammed his pockets full of them.
"Now," said Gretel, "we must escape from the witch's wood."
At last, the wood started to look more and more familiar and soon, in the
distance, they saw their father's house. Then they set off to run home and,
bounding through the open door, fell into the arms of their father.
The woodcutter had not passed a single happy hour since he had left his
children in the wood and his wife, had fallen ill and died. In great
excitement, Gretel shook out her apron. The pearls and
precious stones rolled about the room, and Hansel threw
down one handful after another from his pockets. Their
troubles were at last over and the woodcutter and his
children lived happily ever after.

Jack the Giant-Killer

Once upon a time, in the reign of King Arthur, there lived a wealthy farmer with a son called Jack. In the neighboring county, Mount Macally, there lived a huge and monstrous giant who terrified the local townsfolk. At his approach they would abandon their homes and the giant would seize their cattle, carrying half-a-dozen oxen on his back at a time. As for their sheep and hogs, he would tie them round his waist like a bunch of bananas. Soon the whole area was devastated by his raids.

One day Jack asked the town councillors what reward would be offered to any person destroying the giant. "We would give him the giant's treasure," they said.

"Then I will destroy him," replied Jack.

So he furnished himself with a horn, a shovel, and a pickaxe, and crossed over to the Mount one dark winter's evening. There he fell to work, and before sunrise he had dug a deep pit which he covered over with long sticks and straw. At the break of day, Jack put the horn to his mouth, and blew *"Tantivy"*, *"Tantivy"*. This aroused the giant, who rushed from his cave, crying: "You villain, have you come here to disturb my rest? I will take you whole and broil you for breakfast." No sooner had the giant uttered the words than he tumbled headlong into the pit, which shook the very foundations of the Mount.

Then Jack took his pickaxe and gave the giant a most weighty knock on the very crown of his head, and killed him instantly.

When the local dignitaries heard of his deeds, they declared that Jack should henceforth be given the title, "Jack the Giant-Killer," and they presented him with a sword and an embroidered belt, on which were written these words in letters of gold:

"Here stands our brave and valiant man,
Who slew the giant Cormelian."

The news of Jack's victory soon spread over all the country and a giant, by name of Blunderbore, vowed revenge. Now Jack, some time later, was walking near the very wood inhabited by this giant. Tired and weary, he sat down to rest by the side of a pleasant fountain and soon fell fast asleep. There Blunderbore discovered him, and recognizing Jack, by the lines written on his embroidered belt, he hoisted him onto his shoulders and carried him towards his enchanted castle. The giant locked Jack in an immense chamber full of bones, and went off to fetch a neighbouring giant to share in the boy's destruction. While he was gone, Jack heard a magic voice crying:

"Do what you can to get away,
Or you'll become the giant's prey."

In the corner of the room lay four strong cords. Jack grabbed two of the cords and made a strong noose at the end of each. His window overlooked the castle gate and, as the giants returned, he cast out the ropes, landing one noose over each of their heads. Then, drawing the ends across a beam, he tied them tightly together. Quickly he slid down one of the ropes and as he came face to face with the giants, Jack drew his sword and slew them both. Jack took the giant's keys, unlocked the castle doors and released all the prisoners. He then resumed his journey.

As night fell he came to a large house. He knocked at the gate and there was a monstrous giant with two heads. The giant welcomed Jack jovially and offered him a bed for the night. But in the dead of night Jack heard the giant muttering:

"Though here you lodge with me this night,
You shall not see the morning light."

"So that's what you think," said Jack. He leapt out of bed, stuffed a pillow in his place and hid in a corner of the room. At the dead time

of night in came the giant. He struck several blows on the bed with his club, confident that he had broken every bone in Jack's body. The next morning he was amazed when Jack appeared. "How have you rested?" asked the giant; "did you not feel anything in the night?"

"No," replied Jack, "nothing but a rat, which swished her tail over me two or three times, I believe."

"You must have some breakfast," growled the giant. And he brought Jack a bowl containing four gallons of cold porridge.

"I will trick this wicked giant," thought Jack.

He put a large leather bag under his coat and tipped the porridge into it. Then, telling the giant he had a trick to show him, he took a knife, ripped open the bag, and out poured all the cold porridge. The challenge was too great for the giant to resist.

"Odds splutters, I can do that trick myself!" The monster snatched up a knife, ripped open his belly, and fell down dead.

Now, it happened at that time that King Arthur's only son decided to travel to a neighboring country to rescue a beautiful lady possessed with seven evil spirits. After several days' travel, the prince came to a market-town where he learned that a man had just been arrested for stealing bread. "Let him free," he urged the townsfolk, "this money shall help you to replace the loaf and, indeed, will leave you with money in hand."

Jack who was passing that way was so taken with the generosity of the prince that he asked if he might be his servant. And so the next morning the two men set forth on their journey together. As they rode out of town, an old woman called after the prince: "He owed me two coins these seven years; pray pay me as well as the rest." Putting his hand to his pocket, the prince gave the woman all he had left.

When the sun began to set, the King's son turned to Jack: "Since we now have no money, where shall we lodge this night?"

"Master, we'll do well enough, for I have an uncle lives within two miles of this place; he is a huge and monstrous giant with three heads; I myself will go ahead and prepare the way for you."

Jack rode away full speed and, coming to the gate of the castle, he

knocked with all his might. The giant roared out like thunder: "Who's there?"

"Only your Cousin Jack with bad news, I fear."

"Listen," replied the giant, "I am the giant with three heads, and I can fight five hundred men in armor, and make them flee away as fast as the driven snow,"

"No, uncle, the king's son is on his way with a thousand men in armor to kill you and destroy everything that you have."

"Oh, Cousin Jack," said the giant, "this is bad news indeed. I will hide. Lock, bolt, and bar me in, and keep the keys until the prince is gone." Jack locked up the giant and then fetched his master. That night while the poor giant lay trembling in a vault under the ground, the prince and Jack ate and slept in peace.

Early in the morning Jack sent the prince on in advance while he freed the giant from the vault. The giant asked Jack how he might reward him for keeping the castle from destruction.

"Why" said Jack, "I really want nothing but the old coat and cap, together with the old rusty sword and slippers which are at the head of your bed."

"Take them all," said the giant. "The coat will keep you invisible, the cap will furnish you with knowledge, the sword will cut to pieces whatever you strike. And the shoes are of extraordinary swiftness."

Jack thanked his uncle and left the castle. Soon he had caught up with the prince and the two men travel ed to the house of the enchanted lady. She prepared a splendid banquet but as they finished eating she wiped the prince's mouth with a handkerchief and said: "Show me that handkerchief tomorrow or else you'll lose your head."

In the middle of the night she called upon her evil spirits to carry the handkerchief away but Jack put on his coat of darkness and his shoes of swiftness and followed the evil one to his lair. Jack seized the handkerchief and brought it back to his master, who in the morning showed it to the lady. The next night the same thing happened and she called again to the evil spirit, angry with him for letting the handkerchief go. Jack, the invisible, did not hesitate. He cut off the devil's head and brought it to his master, who the next morning presented it to the lady. Thus the enchantment was broken and the evil spirits left her. Now she appeared in all her beauty and the prince and his lady decided to get married. They returned to the court of King Arthur, where Jack, for his many great exploits, was made a Knight of the Round Table.

Beauty and The Beast

Once upon a time a rich merchant lived in great splendor with his sons and daughters. One day they were struck by terrible misfortune for their house caught fire and, at the same time, the merchant's fleet was destroyed. All that was left to them was a small wooden house in the middle of a dark forest.

After two years, the merchant received news that one of his ships had come safely into port and he set off immediately to claim his cargo. His children were overjoyed and they begged him to bring them back jewels and fine clothes; only the youngest child, called Beauty, did not ask for anything.

"And what shall I bring you, Beauty?"

"There is nothing that I need," she answered.

"But, Beauty, I must bring you something," her father insisted.

She laughed: "Then perhaps you could bring me one single rose."

But when the merchant reached the seaport he found that the report was false. There was no cargo and in great distress he started

the long journey home. Deep
snow and bitter frost hindered his
progress and at night, cold and exhausted, he crouched
in the hollow of a tree and listened to the howling of
wolves. When day broke, his path had become covered
by snow. He was lost.

After many hours the snow suddenly vanished
without warning and the merchant found himself in a
beautiful avenue of orange trees, leading to a most
splendid palace. He walked slowly towards it and
climbed a flight of marble steps.

Inside the palace he passed through
several splendidly furnished rooms
but everywhere he went a deep silence
reigned. At last the merchant found
a small room and there lay down on a
couch in front of a blazing fire. Soon, tired
out, he fell asleep. When he awoke he
saw, close to the couch, a little table
covered with delicious food. He ate in
silence and then wandered back through the
rooms and into the surrounding gardens.

Out in the walled garden the sun shone,
the birds sang, and the flowers bloomed. He
stopped and picked one single red rose for
Beauty but as he did so he heard a strange
rumbling noise. He turned and found
himself face to face with a frightful, angry
Beast.

"Who told you that you might gather my
roses?" the Beast called out in his deep,

echoing voice. "I have sheltered you and fed you. Why do your steal my flowers?" "Pardon me, noble sir," replied the merchant. Then he told the Beast the whole story of his ill fortune.

"I will spare your life on one condition," replied the Beast. "You must bring one of your daughters to live with me."

"But how can I do such a thing?" protested the merchant.

"I give you a month to return with one of your daughters and she must come willingly. Do not imagine that you can hide from me, for if you fail to keep your word I will come and fetch you."

The following day the merchant set out on his journey, riding a white horse given to him by the Beast. When he reached home he presented Beauty with her rose and then told his children all that had happened.

"I am the cause of this misfortune," Beauty said, "for I asked you to pick the rose. I will be the one to return to the castle with you."

One month later, mounted on the back of the white horse, Beauty returned to the palace with her father. There they went straight to the little room where a splendid fire was burning and the table was daintily spread with food. When they had finished their meal they heard the Beast approaching and as he entered the room Beauty struggled to hide her feelings.

"Have you come willingly?" asked the Beast, in a voice that would have struck terror into the boldest heart. Beauty answered bravely that she had indeed come of her own free will.

"I am pleased with you," said the Beast, "as for you, old man," he added, "at sunrise you will take your departure. You will find the white horse waiting to take you home." Then, turning to Beauty, he said: "Take your father into the next room and help him to choose gifts and treasures for your brothers and sisters."

The following morning two horses were waiting, one loaded with treasure. The merchant mounted the first horse and as he turned to say goodbye the horses galloped away at such speed that Beauty lost sight of her father almost instantly.

She wandered sadly back to her own room, and lay down to rest. As she slept she dreamed that she was walking by a brook, overhung with myrtle trees, lamenting her sad fate. There by the stream a most

handsome prince approached her.

"Ah, Beauty! try to find me, no matter how I may be disguised. I love you dearly. In making me happy you will find your own happiness."

"What can I do to make you happy?" replied Beauty.

"Only be grateful," he answered, "and do not trust too much to your eyes."

When Beauty awoke she set out to explore the palace. The first room she entered was lined with mirrors, and Beauty could see herself reflected on every side. In one mirror she caught sight of a bracelet hanging from a chandelier. To her great surprise she found that it held a portrait of the Prince who had appeared in her dream. She slipped the bracelet onto her arm and flung open the doors leading to the next room, a gallery hung with splendid pictures. Immediately she was drawn towards a portrait of the same handsome prince. Beauty then explored a room containing every musical instrument imaginable and after, when she grew tired of playing and singing, she opened a door leading to a vast library. So many books! It would take her a lifetime to read them. As darkness fell, wax candles in candlesticks of diamonds and rubies lit up the library and Beauty returned to her room.

In silence she ate the meal prepared for her but, as she finished, she heard the Beast's footsteps approaching. He greeted her in his gruff, deep voice and Beauty told him how she had passed the day. When he got up to leave he asked: "Do you love me, Beauty? Will you marry me? Do not fear to say 'yes' or 'no'."

"Oh no, Beast," said Beauty hastily, quite taken aback.

That night Beauty dreamed once more of her unknown prince. Why was she so unkind to him, he asked her. Her dream merged into another dream, then another, but in each one her charming prince was present.

The following morning Beauty decided to amuse herself in the garden, for the sun was shining and the cool fountains were playing. Everything was strangely familiar to her and in her wanderings she came to the brook where the myrtle trees grew and where she had first met the prince in her dream.

Each day Beauty made new discoveries; a room full of silks and ribbons one day, an aviary of rare birds the next. Best of all, a room with magic windows where, before her eyes, a pantomime was acted out, with dances and colored lights and music.

Every evening after supper the Beast came to visit her and asked her to marry him. Each evening she refused his offer.

After a time Beauty began to long for the company of her father and her brothers and sisters and she asked the Beast if she might visit them. He sighed mournfully but nevertheless agreed to let her go for two months: "Return when your time is up or you will have cause to repent. If you do not come your faithful Beast will be dead."

When Beauty awoke the next morning she was in an oddly familiar room. She rushed out to greet her father and to hug her brothers and sisters. Beauty was overjoyed to be with her family but she often found her thoughts returning to the Beast. Two months passed by but her family could not bear to let her go. One night she had a most dismal dream in which she wandered along a lonely path in the palace gardens. She heard terrible groans and found the Beast stretched out upon his side, apparently dying.

The following day she announced to her family that she must return to the palace. That night she turned her ring round and round upon her finger, as instructed, and said in a clear voice: "I wish to go back to my palace and see my Beast again." She fell asleep instantly and awoke in the palace.

But in the evening the Beast failed to appear and Beauty was terrified. Up and down the paths and avenues she ran, calling in vain, until at last she stopped for a minute's rest and found herself standing opposite a shady path. Hurrying down the path she came to a cave in which lay the Beast, asleep, so Beauty thought. She approached and stroked his head, but he did not move. She ran to fetch some water which she sprinkled over his face. As he began to revive she cried: "Oh, Beast, how your frightened me! I never knew how much I cared for you until I feared I was too late to save your life."

"Beauty, you came only just in time. I was dying because I thought you had forgotten your promise. Go back now to the palace and I shall meet you there."

Beauty returned to the palace and when the Beast came he asked, as he had so often before: "Beauty, will you marry me?" This time she answered softly: "Yes, dear Beast." As she spoke a blaze of light lit up the windows of the palace; fireworks crackled and guns fired and across the avenue of orange-trees, in letters made of fireflies,

were the words: "Long live the prince and his bride."

Turning to ask the Beast what was the meaning of all this, Beauty found that, in his place, there stood the prince of her dreams! At the same moment the wheels of a chariot clattered on the terrace and two ladies entered the room. One turned to Beauty: "How can I thank you enough for rescuing my son from this terrible enchantment." And then she tenderly embraced the prince and Beauty.

The marriage was celebrated the very next day with the utmost splendor, and Beauty and the prince lived happily ever after.

Snow-white and Rose-red

Once upon a time there was a poor widow who lived in a little cottage with her two children, Snow-white and Rose-red. The two sisters loved each other dearly and they were the sweetest and best children in the whole world.

Snow-white and Rose-red often roamed alone through the woods gathering berries, feeding animals and birds: the little rabbit would nibble at a cabbage leaf from their hands, and the birds would sing to them. One evening

they decided to sleep in the woods, and when it grew dark they lay
down together and fell into a deep sleep.

In the morning, just as the sun rose in the sky, they saw, standing
close by, a child dressed in a shimmering white robe. The child smiled
sweetly at them but spoke not a word before he vanished into the wood.
Snow-white and Rose-red were frightened – for they realized that they had
been sleeping close to the edge of a great cliff.

When they returned home they told their mother about the child and
the cliff. She smiled: "The angel who looks after good children has
been watching over you."

One winter evening there was a knock at the door. Rose-red drew back
the bolt and there, standing in the darkness, was a poor, dishevelled man.
Yet this was no man – it was a bear who poked his thick brown head
around the door. Rose-red screamed aloud and sprang back in terror.
Immediately the bear began to reassure her: "Don't be afraid, I won't hurt
you. I am half-frozen and only wish to warm myself a little."

"Poor bear," said the mother, "lie down by the fire." The bear asked
the children to beat the snow from his fur, and they scrubbed him
until he was dry. Then he stretched himself in front of the fire.

The children loved playing with the big brown bear, they tugged at his fur, plonked their feet on his back, and rolled him about hither and thither. When it was bedtime the mother turned to the bear and said: "You can stay here and take shelter."

In the morning, when the children unbolted the door, the bear trotted out of the house and back into the wood. But from that day onwards, the bear came every evening at the same hour and played with the children, then lay down by the hearth.

When spring came and all outside was green, the bear said: "Now I must go away and leave you for the summer."

"Don't go, dear bear. Why must you leave us?" asked Snow-white.

"I need to protect my treasure for wicked dwarfs desire to steal it. In winter, when the earth is frozen hard, they stay underground. But now the sun has warmed the earth, they reappear and steal anything that is precious." Snow-white and Rose-red were sad. They said good-bye and Snow-white unbolted the door. As she did so, the bear caught a piece of his fur in the door-knocker and Snow-white thought she spied the sparkle of glittering gold beneath his fur.

One spring day, the mother sent her children out to gather sticks for the fire. In a clearing in the wood, they came upon a big tree trunk

stretched right across their path. There, in the long grass they saw a squat dwarf with a wizened face and a long flowing beard. The end of his beard was jammed into a cleft of the tree, and the little man was tugging hard, like a dog on a chain. He glared at the girls with his fiery red eyes and screamed out: "What are you doing you ninnies? Can't you help me?"

"What's the matter, little man?" asked Rose-red innocently.

"You stupid, inquisitive goose!" replied the dwarf, "I was trying to split this log but the wood was so slippery my wedge fell out of the cleft; I am stuck fast by my beard." The children pulled and pulled but it was no good.

"I've got just the thing," said Snow-white as she took out her scissors and snipped off the end of his beard. "You horrid wretches, cutting off a piece of my splendid beard. What cheek!" muttered the dwarf as he seized a bag full of gold hidden in the grass, and disappeared.

A few days later Snow-white and Rose-red went to the stream to catch some fish. When they got there they saw an enormous grasshopper spring toward the water. They ran forward eagerly but whom should it turn out to be but that wizened old dwarf. "Where are you off to?" asked Rose-red, "you're surely not going to jump into the water?"

"I'm not such a fool," screamed the dwarf. "Can't you see that that fish is trying to pull me in?"

The dwarf had hooked a big fish and his long beard had got caught up in his line. The girls held him firm and tried to help but they could not free him and so out came the scissors and snip. "You toadstools!" he yelled. "How dare you disfigure me so. I can't appear like this. You horrid interfering little girls!" He stormed off to the nearby rushes, snatched up a sack of pearls and disappeared.

Soon after this Snow-white and Rose-red went to the market town to buy some ribbons and lace. As they were walking along, they saw a great bird slowly circling above them. Suddenly the bird swooped down and pounced on something hidden behind a rock. There was a sharp cry. The children ran forward and there, caught in the talons of the eagle, was the nasty little dwarf. They grabbed his coat and pulled and pulled and finally the eagle let go.

"Treat me more carefully!" screeched the ungrateful fellow. "You have torn my clothes to pieces, you good-for-nothings." And he picked up a bag of gold and vanished under a rock. On their way home Snow-white and Rose-red met the dwarf once more. He was crouched over a mound of dazzling jewels. The children could hardly take their eyes off them. "What are you standing gaping at my stones for?" screamed the dwarf, scarlet with rage. But he was interrupted by a deep

growling noise and a big, brown bear ran out from behind a rock.

"Dear bear!" whined the evil dwarf, "Spare me, spare me. Take all my treasure and look, eat up these two wicked girls – tasty morsels I'd say."

The bear paid no attention but struck the dwarf one mighty blow with his paw and the wizened creature never moved again. The girls fled in terror but the bear called after them: "Snow-white, Rose-red, don't be afraid. Wait." They recognized the bear's voice and as he came towards them the bear's fur fell off and before them they saw a handsome prince all dressed in cloth of gold.

"I am a king's son," he told the girls, "doomed to wander the woods as a bear until I could catch and kill that evil dwarf, when the curse would be lifted and I would be myself again."

Snow-white married the prince and Rose-red his brother and between them they divided the great treasure. The mother came to live with her children and in the garden she planted two rose trees, one white and one red.

The Tinder Box

Once upon a time there was a soldier who came marching along the highway. One, two! One, two! He had been to the wars and he was on his way home. On the road he met an old witch; she was so ugly her lower lip hung right down to her chin. "Good evening soldier!" she said. "What a nice sword you've got and such a big knapsack. You're a real soldier. You shall have as much money as you wish." "Thank you, old witch," answered the soldier. "See that big tree," said the witch, "it is

hollow inside! Climb up
and you will see a hole going right down
under the tree! Let yourself down and I will
haul you up again when you call."

"What for?" asked the soldier.

"To fetch money!" said the witch. "When you
get down to the bottom of the tree you will find
a wide passage with three doors. Go into the first
room and you will find a big box in the middle of the
floor. A dog is sitting on top of it, and he has eyes as
big as saucers. Spread my blue-checked apron out
on the floor; pick up the dog, put him on it, open
the box and take out as much money as you like. It
is all copper, but if you like silver, go into the next
room. There you will find a dog with eyes as big as
millstones. Put him on my apron and take the
money. If you prefer gold you can have it too, and
as much as you can carry. The gold is in the box in
the third room. But the dog
sitting on that box has eyes as
big as the Round Tower. He
is a dog indeed. But don't
let it trouble you. Just put
him on my apron and then
he won't hurt you, and
you can take as much
gold out of the box as
you like!"

"That's easy enough,"
said the soldier, "but
what am I to give you
old witch? for you'll

want something."

"No," said the witch, "not a single penny. I only want you to bring up the old tinder box that my grandmother forgot last time she was down there!"

"In that case, tie a rope round my waist," said the soldier. "Here you are," said the witch, "and here is my checked apron." Then the soldier climbed up the tree, let himself slide down the hollow trunk, and found himself in the wide passage where many hundreds of lamps were burning. He opened the first door. Ugh! There sat the dog with eyes as big as saucers staring at him.

"You're a nice fellow," said the soldier, as he put him on the witch's apron, and he took as many pennies as he could cram in his pockets. Then he shut the box, put the dog back on top of it again, and went into the next room. There sat the dog with eyes as big as millstones. He put that dog on the apron but when he saw all the silver in the box he threw away the coppers and stuffed his pockets and his knapsack with silver. Then he went into the third room. Oh! how horrible! That dog really had eyes as big as the Round Tower, eyes that rolled round and round like wheels.

"Good evening, dog," said the soldier saluting.

Then he lifted the dog down onto the apron and opened the chest. What a pile of gold! he could buy the whole city with it, and all the sugar-pigs from the

cake women, and all the rocking-horses in the world!

So the soldier threw away the silver and put gold in its place. He crammed his pockets with so much gold he could hardly walk! He put the dog back on the box, shut the door, and shouted up the tree: "Haul me up, you old witch!"

"Have you got the tinder box?"

"Oh! to be sure," said the soldier. "I had quite forgotten it." And he went back to fetch it. Then the witch hauled him up, and there he was standing on the high road with his pockets, boots, knapsack and cap, full of gold.

"What do you want the tinder box for?" asked the soldier.

"Mind you own business," said the witch.

"You've got the money, give it to me!"

"No!" said the soldier. "Tell me directly what you want with it, or I will draw my sword and cut off your head."

"I won't!" said the witch.

So the soldier cut off her head – there she lay dead! The soldier then tied all the money up in her apron, put the tinder box in his pocket, and marched off to the town.

It was a beautiful town, and he went to the finest hotel, ordered the grandest rooms and all the food he liked best. Next day he bought new boots and splendid clothes, and became a fine gentleman. The people told him all about the grand things in their town, and about their king and the lovely princess, his daughter.

"Where can I see her?" asked the soldier. "You can't see her at all," they replied, "she lives in a great copper castle surrounded with walls. Nobody but the king goes in and out, for it has been foretold that she will marry a soldier, and the king doesn't like that."

The soldier now led a merry life. He went to the theatres, drove about in the park, and gave away money to the poor. He wore fine clothes, and had many friends. But as he went on spending money every day he soon found himself with only two coins left. He had to move out of his fine rooms. He took a tiny attic up many stairs and none of his friends ever came to see him. One dark evening when he had not even enough money to buy a candle, he suddenly remembered that there was a small candle in the old tinder box he had brought out of the hollow tree. He got out the tinder box and struck fire, but, as the sparks flew out from the flint, the door burst open and the dog with eyes as big as saucers stood before him and said: "What does my lord command?" "By heaven," said the soldier, "this is a nice kind of tinder box. Get me some money." The dog vanished and was back in a twinkling with a big bag full of pennies in its mouth. Now the soldier found what a treasure he had in the tinder box. If he struck once, the dog which sat on the box of copper came; if he struck twice, the dog on the silver box came; and if he struck three times, the dog guarding the box of gold came. He moved back to his grand rooms with all his fine clothes and all his friends came back to see him.

Suddenly, he began to think. It was a curious thing that no man could ever see the princess. What was the good of her beauty if she was always shut up in that copper palace. The soldier struck the flint, and, *whisk*, came the dog with eyes as big as saucers.

"I know that it is the middle of the night," said the soldier," but I am very anxious to see the princess if

only for a moment."
The dog was out of the door in an instant, and before the soldier had time to think, he returned with the princess. There she was, fast asleep on the dog's back, and she was so lovely that anyone could see that she was a real princess. The soldier kissed her for he was a true soldier.
Then the dog ran back with the princess, but in the morning, when the king and queen were having breakfast, the princess said she had had a wonderful dream about a dog and a soldier. She had ridden on the dog's back and the soldier had kissed her.
"That's a pretty tale," said the queen, but she made an old lady in waiting sit by her daughter's bed that night.
The soldier longed to see the princess again and the next night he sent the dog to fetch her. But, when the dog appeared, the lady in waiting ran behind them and she

made a big cross on the gate of the soldier's house. When the dog took the princess back to the palace he saw the cross and he made crosses on all the gates in the town.
When the queen heard about all this she determined she would discover what

was happening. She made a pretty little bag of silk, which she filled with wheat. She stitched it to the princess's nightgown and she cut a small hole in it so that the grains would drop out to show where the princess went. The dog never noticed the grains and the next morning when the king and queen saw where the trail had finished they seized the soldier and commanded that he be thrown into the dungeons. There he lay for months. Then one day they said to him: "Tomorrow you will be hanged."

That morning he could see through the bars of his cell window the people hurrying out of town to see him hanged. Everyone was going; among them was a shoemaker's boy in his leather apron and slippers. He was in such a hurry that he lost one of his slippers, and it fell under the soldier's window. "I say, you boy! Don't be in such a hurry," said the soldier to him. "Nothing will happen until I get there. But if you run to the house where I live, and fetch me my tinder box, I will give you a gold coin!"

The boy tore off, got the tinder box and gave it to the soldier.

Now – outside the town a high scaffold had been erected, surrounded by crowds of people. The king and queen sat on a throne opposite the judges and councillors. The soldier mounted the scaffold but just as they were putting the rope around his neck he asked the king whether he could, as one final favor on earth, smoke one last pipe. The king could not deny him this, so the soldier took out his tinder box and struck fire, once, twice, three times, and there were all the dogs. The one with eyes like saucers, the one with eyes like millstones, and the one with eyes as big as the Round Tower.

"Help me! Save me from being hanged!" cried the soldier. So the dogs rushed at the hangman and the guards and the councillors, and they took one by his legs, and one by his nose, and they threw them up so high in the air that when they came down they were all broken into small pieces.

"No!" cried the king as the biggest dog seized him and the queen at the same time. But the dog just tossed them in the air.

Then everyone shouted: "Good soldier, save us! You shall be our king and marry the princess."

So the soldier was conducted to the king's chariot and the three dogs danced in front of him shouting "Hurrah!". The boys all whistled and the soldiers presented arms. The princess came out of the copper palace and she became queen and that pleased her very much. The wedding took place that week and all the dogs

came and sat at a special table with their
eyes staring and going round and round.

The Three Little Pigs

Once upon a time there were three little pigs who went out into the world to seek their fortune and build their own houses.

The first little pig met a man carrying a bundle of straw: "Please, man, give me some straw to build me a house," he asked. The man gave him some straw, and the little pig built his house. Presently along came a wolf who knocked loudly at the door and called: "Little pig, little pig, let me come in."

And the little pig squealed: "No, no, by the hair of my chinny, chin chin!"

The wolf replied: "Then I'll huff and I'll puff and I'll blow your house in."

So he huffed, and he puffed, and he blew the house in, and gobbled up that little pig.

The second little pig jogged along and met a man carrying a bundle of wood: "Please man, give me some wood to build me a house," and the man gave him some wood, and the little pig built his house.

Then along came the wolf, who

called out: "Little pig, little pig, let me come in."

"No, no, by the hair of my chinny, chin chin," squealed this little pig.

"Then I'll puff, and I'll huff, and I'll blow your house in."

So he huffed, and he puffed, and he blew the wooden house down, and gobbled up the second pig.

The third little pig met a man carrying a load of bricks: "Please, man, give me those bricks to build me a house." So the man gave him the bricks, and this pig built a fine house. Presently the wolf came along and said: "Little pig, little pig, let me come in."

"No, no, by the hair of my chinny chin chin."

"Then I'll huff, and I'll puff, and I'll blow your house in."

Well, he huffed, and he puffed, and he puffed and he huffed, but he could NOT blow the brick house down. The wolf then decided to trick the little pig so he said: "Little pig, I know where there is a nice field of turnips."

"Where?" asked this little pig.

"Oh, in Farmer Smith's field, and tomorrow morning we will go together and get some of these turnips for dinner."

"Very well," said the little pig, "What time do you intend to set off?" "Six o'clock is turnip-picking time," replied the wolf. But this little pig got up at five o'clock and gathered the turnips before the wolf came. When the wolf arrived he called out: "Little pig, are you ready?"

"Ready!" exclaimed the little pig, "I have been and come back again, and got myself a nice potful for dinner, thank you."

The wolf was very angry, but he still believed that he could trick the little pig. "Little Pig, I know where there is a nice apple tree," he said. "Where?" said the pig.

"Down at Merry Orchard," replied the wolf, "I will come for you at five o'clock in the morning."

The little pig set out at four o'clock in the morning, hoping to get back before the wolf's visit. But the journey was long, and he also had to climb the apple tree. Just as he was scrambling down he spied the wolf who jumped up at the tree and snarled: "Little pig, I see that you are here before me. Tell me, are those apples tasty?"

"Extremely tasty," the little pig assured him, "I will throw one down for you so you can taste one for yourself." He threw the apple right down the hill so, while the wolf was chasing it, the little pig jumped down and ran home safely. The next day the wolf came again, and said to the little pig: "Little pig, there is a fair in the town this afternoon. Will you go?" "Oh, yes," said the little pig, "certainly. What time will you be ready?"

"At three o'clock precisely," said the wolf. So the little pig went off at two o'clock and bought a butter-churn at the fair. Just as he was heading for home with the churn he spied the wolf. The little pig scrambled into the churn, and rolled down the hill inside it. The wolf was terrified by the churn and ran all the way home without even stopping to visit the fair. When he returned to the little pig's house, the little pig laughed at him. "Ha! Ha! You were really frightened. It was me inside that butter churn, rumbling and rolling down the hill."

The wolf was white with rage. He sprang onto the roof to get down the chimney. But the pig had a large pot boiling on the fire and as the wolf came down he took off the lid and – SPLASH – in fell the wolf. The little pig popped on the cover again, boiled up the wolf, and ate him for supper. And, of course, this little pig lived happily ever after.

The Frogs Choose

There was a time when the frogs had no king, but lived
in the lakes in perfect freedom. They got tired of this
though, and asked Jupiter, their God, to give them a
king so that they could be ruled properly, with rewards
and punishments. Jupiter listened, and threw a log into
their lake to be king. It made a fearful splash and they were
terrified and hid in the mud. Then one bold frog took a
look at this new king, decided there was nothing to fear and
jumped on top of him. And so did all the other frogs. Then
they complained to Jupiter that this king was too boring
and they wanted another. So Jupiter sent them another
king in the shape of a great big stork, who took away their
freedom and their possessions and attacked them. They
complained again, but this time Jupiter sent back a
message, saying: 'If you will not be content
when all is going well, then you must be
patient when things go wrong. You were
better off with the log.' And the moral of
this story is if you change things just for the
sake of changing them, you may well end up
worse off.

a King

Town Mouse and Country Mouse

Once upon a time there were two cousins, a Town Mouse, and a Country Mouse. The Country Mouse lived in a hole directly beneath a grassy bank. In one corner of her little hole stood her bed, made from scrumpled up newspaper and twigs; in another lay her hoard of nuts, and odd bits and pieces.

One day Country Mouse was delighted to receive a visit from her cousin, the Town Mouse. But Town Mouse was rather grumpy after her long trek and squeaked indignantly at her cousin: "Do you really live in a dark little hole, can this be your *real* home?"

Country Mouse was most upset. "It's all my own," she replied, "I've got everything I need here."

"It's fit only for beetles and ants," muttered Town Mouse as she surveyed the little hole. "You've got no idea what it is like in my house. Fine rooms, corridors to race down, each day a feast of crumbs under the dining room table."

"My food is delicious too," interrupted

Country Mouse as she scuttled away to her larder. "Dear cousin, take a nibble at this fine apple core or perhaps you would prefer to gnaw at one of my rinds of cheese."

"*Rind* did you say? In my house there's a larder as big as your mouse hole piled high with cheeses – whole ones, holey ones, soft ones, hard ones, smelly ones – you've simply no idea. I'll just munch a few of your nuts," said Town Mouse.

Then she turned to Country Mouse: "Now listen, I simply cannot stay here a moment longer. You must accompany me, *dear* cousin, to my house. You'll soon see how we mice really live."

Off they set through the fields and lanes and came, at last, to the town. "Ordinary houses," muttered Town Mouse as they scurried along, "wait until you see *my* house."

A short time later they came to a grand house. Town Mouse led the way under the door, through the hall and along the passage. Finally they reached the larder. Country Mouse's whiskers were quivering and twitching with excitement as she spied first a great smoked ham, then piles of apples, and giant cheeses.

Country Mouse scuttled towards the cheese as Town Mouse squeaked: "Keep away, there's a trap that'll snap you in two. Scramble up on the shelf. It's safe there."

Suddenly the door opened: "Quick, hide, it's the cook," whispered Town Mouse, and the two mice scurried behind a great jar of pickles.

"Mice!" muttered the cook. "Puss, puss," he shouted through the open door, "catch those horrors at once, or there will be no supper for you."

The door slammed shut and the great ginger tom leapt onto a shelf. The two mice dived onto the floor to escape and as the cat jumped down he could see Town Mouse's tail disappearing into a hole in the wainscot. But poor Country Mouse was not so lucky. She panicked, and slithered this way and that and the cat pounced on her, let her go, and pounced again. He drove her right up to the open hole but, as he lifted his paw, Country Mouse darted into the hole, safe at last. A few minutes later she peeped out, saw the ginger tom lapping up his saucer of milk, and bolted for the door. She squeezed under it and ran all the way home. She looked around her cosy hole before snuggling down contentedly on her bed of newspaper and twigs. How much better was her own simple home than all the luxuries of town life!

Aladdin

Once upon a time there lived a poor tailor with a son called Aladdin, a lazy young lad who spent all his time idling about the streets. One day a stranger approached him and asked whether he was, by chance, the son of Mustapha. "I am indeed," replied Aladdin, surprised by the stranger's question, "but my father is dead and has been for many years."

On hearing Aladdin's words, the stranger embraced him warmly and patted him on the back: "Wonderful, wonderful, my boy!" he exclaimed, putting his arm around Aladdin's shoulder. "Here I am at last, your long-lost uncle. Please do me a favour. Run and tell your mother I am here. This evening I shall come to dine with her."

Now this stranger was no relation of Aladdin's. He was a famous African magician who wanted Aladdin for his own purposes, as we shall see.

That evening the magician, laden down with wine and fruit, presented himself at Aladdin's house. His poor mother was delighted and believed the magician actually was her long lost brother-in-law. Later that evening, when he learned that Aladdin was an idle rascal who scampered off at the very mention of work, the magician rounded on him: "Come, come, boy, no son of my dear departed brother can be left to twiddle his thumbs. There's plenty for a bright young fellow like you to do. Tut, tut." "Indeed," he went on, waving his arms about, "I've got just the trade for you! I'll set you up in a shop, stock it with exotic fruits and spices and in no time you'll be the smartest shopkeeper in town." Aladdin and his mother couldn't believe their luck and when, in the morning, the magician appeared with a fine suit of clothes for Aladdin their happiness was complete. The following day the magician asked Aladdin to join him on an important expedition. Then he led Aladdin out through the city gates right into the heart of the countryside. In the heat of the day they stopped to eat some bread and, as they munched away, the magician pointed to the steep mountains facing them and told Aladdin that there the expedition would end. On and on they walked and when, at last, they reached the two mountains, divided by a narrow valley, the magician became very agitated and shouted at Aladdin: "Gather up some sticks, my boy. We shall light a fire

and then go about our business."
Aladdin did as he was told and
watched the magician light his
fire. Then the magician sprinkled
some strange smelling powder
over the flames, murmuring as he
did so. Suddenly the earth started
to shake and tremble; a great
gashing hole opened before him.
Aladdin was terrified. He could
hardly bear to look at the empty
hole. Turning, he started to run
away but the magician grasped
his arm and pointed to a square
flat stone with a brass ring
embedded in it: "Beneath this
stone lies treasure. It is yours,
no one else may touch it.
Stop this shivering and
shaking and pull that ring in
front of you."

Aladdin lifted up the stone
without difficulty. There,
before him, lay a flight of
uneven stone steps. The
magician, in an excitable mood,
shouted: "Get down there and at
the foot of the steps you will find
an open door leading into three
vast underground halls. Don't
touch anything or you will
instantly die. These halls lead
out into a garden of trees laden
with fruit. Walk out towards the
lighted lamp. Pour its oil onto
the path and return to me with
this lamp." Then from his finger

he pulled a jewelled ring and presented it to Aladdin.

Well, Aladdin did exactly as he was told, stopping only to pick a little fruit on the way which he stuffed into his pockets. At the mouth of the cave he called out: "Uncle, I've got the lamp!"

"Give it to me, give it to me," shouted the magician impatiently.

"Just wait now, Uncle," teased Aladdin clasping the lamp tightly in his arms. The thwarted magician flew into a violent rage, chucked the rest of his powder on to the dying flames of the fire, muttering angrily. At once the stone above Aladdin's head rolled back into place.

It was dark, very dark in the musty cave and for two days Aladdin groped around in the black hole. At last he rubbed the ring on his finger. A large and frightening genie appeared in a burst of light, and piped out in a thin, silvery voice: "I am the slave of the ring. What do you want." "Let me out of here," gasped Aladdin. At once the stone rolled back and Aladdin scrambled out. Soon he was on his way back to the city. Entering his house he ran to his mother and showed her the lamp. As he took the fruit from his pocket, he told her what had happened. "Sell the lamp and buy some food for us," Aladdin then advised her, and she set about cleaning the lamp. At once a hideous genie appeared.

"What do you want?" it squawked.

"Food, food. Fetch me something to eat!" Aladdin replied, realizing that the lamp, too, possessed magical powers. In a flash, the genie was back, this time with a silver bowl, twelve silver plates containing rich meats, two silver cups, and two bottles of wine.

And for some years Aladdin and his mother lived by the magical powers of the lamp and the gold ring. Then, one day, Aladdin happened to catch a glimpse of the Sultan's daughter through a crack in the palace wall. So beautiful was she, he fell in love with her instantly. That evening Aladdin begged his mother to present herself to the Sultan and to ask him to give his daughter's hand in marriage to Aladdin.

And so Aladdin's mother found herself carrying the magic fruits from the enchanted garden to the Sultan's palace. After a week waiting for an audience she presented the dazzling jewels to the Sultan and made her request. Deeply moved, he turned to her and said: "So great is the love of your son for my daughter, so dazzling the jewels he has bestowed upon me, he is indeed worthy to be my son-in-law." But one of his listening courtiers persuaded the Sultan to postpone the marriage for three months; he wanted his own son to marry the princess. Aladdin's mother was, therefore, bidden to return to the palace with her son three months hence.

Some weeks later Aladdin's mother learned that the Sultan's daughter was to marry the son of the courtier that very day. Aladdin was beside himself with grief. He picked up the lamp, rubbed it, and commanded the genie to bring the bride and bridegroom to him. That night their bed was transported to his room. The bridegroom was forced out into the bitter cold while Aladdin explained to the terrified princess that she was really his wife, promised to him by her father. At dawn the shivering bridegroom and the Sultan's daughter were transported back to the palace.

The Sultan was alarmed at the sight of his pale and miserable daughter. At last she related the strange story to him. "A dream, a dream," her father assured her, but that night the same thing happened, and again the following night. The courtier's son said he would rather die than spend another such fearful night, and asked to be separated from the Sultan's daughter. His wish was granted, and there was an end of feasting and rejoicing.

When the three months were over Aladdin sent his mother to remind the Sultan of his promise: "Good woman, a Sultan must remember his promises, but tell your son to send me forty gold bowls brimful of jewels.

And so Aladdin summoned the genie and, in a flash, forty servants stood before him. As they set out to the palace, two by two, carrying on their heads gold basins filled with sparkling jewels, crowds formed to witness the procession. The Sultan was beside himself with delight: "Good woman, return and tell your son that I wait for him with open arms." Aladdin, when he heard this, summoned the genie and requested a magnificent horse, twenty servants, a gown embroidered with gold thread, and ten thousand pieces of gold.

When the Sultan set eyes on Aladdin, he embraced him and nodded as Aladdin told him that he would build a palace for his princess. At home, once more, Aladdin turned to the genie: "Build me a palace of the finest

marble, set with jasper, agate, and other precious stones."

The very next day Aladdin's palace stood in all its splendour overlooking the town.

But far away in Africa the magician remembered Aladdin and by his magic arts discovered what had happened. He vowed to get hold of the lamp and returned to the old city to carry out his plan. The scheming fellow wasted no time in buying a dozen copper lamps which he marched with to the palace, crying: "New lamps for old! New lamps for old!" The princess was enthralled by this idea and told her servant to fetch Aladdin's old lamp from a corner of his study. Together they presented it to the magician in exchange for a fine new lamp. The magician snatched the magic lamp and hurried away.

Through the city gates the magician ran and on to a deserted encampment where he remained till nightfall. Then he pulled the lamp out of his sack and rubbed it vigorously. The genie popped up and at the magician's command carried him, together with the palace and the princess, to a lonely, sandswept plain in North Africa.

The following morning the Sultan happened to look out of the window towards Aladdin's palace. He could not believe his eyes. Nothing! Nothing at all! He called for his chief courtier who protested that Aladdin was an enchanter. The Sultan, on hearing these words ordered his cavalry to set out and to capture Aladdin.

That evening Aladdin was brought before the Sultan who ordered his head to be cut off. And, as the Sultan shouted: "Where is my daughter – where is your palace?" Aladdin realised what had come to pass. He begged time to find the princess. "Forty days I will give you and if you fail in your task then you will certainly lose your head."

Aladdin was quite distraught. After two days spent wandering about in a dazed state he was so exhausted his hands began to tremble. He looked down at them and the gleaming stone in his ring caught his eye. The ring! Suddenly he remembered. He rubbed his finger hard and amidst a puff of smoke the genie appeared: "Take me to my palace and set me down under my wife's window," Aladdin pleaded.

He fell into a deep sleep and awoke under the princess' window just as her servant was opening the window. The girl immediately informed the princess who ran out to greet him. For a while they were overcome with joy but Aladdin did not forget their danger: "Quick, tell me,

what has become of the old lamp in the corner of my dressing room."

"The African magician who is trying to win my affection carries it about with him," replied the princess sorrowfully.

"Trust me," Aladdin said, "for I must get the lamp. Persuade the magician to dine with you and prepare to put on your most splendid gown. I will return shortly and tell you what you must do."

When Aladdin returned having purchased a particular powder in the town, he gave the princess her instructions. In the evening, the magician was astonished to see the princess dressed so sumptuously and pleasantly surprised to hear her declare that, since Aladdin must be dead, she would welcome his company. "Pray let us celebrate this joyous occasion," she declared as she handed him a goblet in which she had placed Aladdin's powder. He raised it to his lips, took a hearty sip and fell down dead, quite dead.

And now Aladdin lost no time in recovering the lamp and in summoning the genie to carry the palace and all therein back to their own city. The following day the Sultan glanced sorrowfully out of his window. Lo and behold there stood Aladdin's palace as if nothing at all had happened. He hastened to greet his daughter and from her learned of the evil intentions of the magician and of his timely death. At once the Sultan proclaimed a week of celebration and feasting for all his peoples. Some years later Aladdin became Sultan and reigned wisely for many years, encouraging his subjects in the ways of hard work, for he never forgot his own idle youth.

The Little Mermaid

Once upon a time far out to sea where the water is as blue as the brightest cornflower and as clear as the purest crystal, there dwelt the Mermen, and in the deepest part of the ocean lay the palace of the Merman King. The king's palace was surrounded by the most wonderful trees and plants, its walls formed of coral, and its long pointed windows carved from the clearest amber. Its roof was tiled with mussel shells, a gleaming pearl set in each one.

The Merman King had for many years been a widower and he had six daughters who were all lovely, but the youngest daughter was the prettiest of all. Her skin was as soft and delicate as a rose petal and her eyes as blue as the depths of the sea. Like all mermaids she possessed, in place of legs and feet, a fish's tail.

Nothing pleased the youngest princess more than to hear about the world of human beings living above the sea. She listened intently to her grandmother's stories of towns and people, animals and flowers. "When you are fifteen you will be allowed to rise up from the sea and sit on the rocks in the moonlight, and look at the big ships sailing by, and you too will see the woods and towns."

But there were five whole years to wait before she could rise from the bottom of the sea. Many a night the little mermaid stood by the open windows and looked up through the dark blue water, which the fish lashed with their tails and fins, and gazed at the far-off moon and the stars.

By now the eldest princess had reached her fifteenth birthday and could venture above the water. When she returned she had hundreds of things to tell them, but the most delightful of all, she said, was to lie in the moonlight on a sandbank and gaze at the large town close to the shore, where the lights twinkled like hundreds

of stars. How eagerly the young princess listened to her sister's tales. When later in the evening she stood at the open window and looked up through the dark blue water, she thought of the big town with all its noise and bustle, and fancied that she could even hear church bells ringing.

The next year the second sister rose to the surface of the sea just as the sun was setting on the horizon. It was, she declared, the most beautiful sight that she had ever seen. The sky was like gold, the clouds floated in red and violet splendour over her head and a flock of wild swans flew like a long white veil over the water towards the setting sun; she swam towards the sun, but it sank, and all the rosy light on cloud and water faded away.

When it was the third sister's turn she ventured up a river and looked at the beautiful green vine-clad hills and saw palaces and grand houses peeping through splendid woods. In a tiny bay she found a group of little children running about naked and paddling in the water. She called to them but they were frightened and ran away.

The fourth sister was not so bold; she stayed in the remotest part of the ocean where she could see for miles and miles around her, and stare at the sky above which looked, she thought, like a great glass dome.

Now it was the fifth sister's turn. It was winter and the sea was green with large icebergs floating on its surface. They looked like pearls, she said, with the most wonderful shapes and sparkled like diamonds. She sat down to rest on a floating iceberg but as evening approached the sky became overcast and a storm erupted. She listened to the thunder and watched the blue lightning flash in zigzags down on the shining sea.

At last it was the little mermaid's turn and through the water she rose, as lightly and airily as a bubble. The sun had just set as her head emerged above the water, the clouds still lighted with a rose and golden splendour and the air mild and fresh. A large three-masted ship lay close by. There was music and singing on board and as darkness fell hundreds of gaily coloured lanterns were lighted.

The little mermaid swam right up to the cabin windows and looked through at the crowds of gaily-dressed people. She gazed at the handsome young prince in whose honour these festivities were taking place. Suddenly hundreds of fireworks erupted and so frightened her that she dived under the

water. As she rose again it seemed as though all the stars of heaven were falling in showers around about her. Great suns whirled round, fire-fish hung in the blue air. It grew late but still the little mermaid was mesmerised by the ship and the beautiful prince.

Suddenly a violent storm blew up and the little mermaid found herself buffeted by waves. The ship heaved and listed in the angry sea. Black waves rose like mountains and broke over its decks, snapping the main mast like a reed.

As it split asunder the little mermaid saw that the prince was drowning. She swam towards him. He was unconscious as she held his head above the water and allowed the waves to drive them hither and thither throughout the long night. At daybreak she could see the shoreline covered with beautiful green woods. She swam towards it and placed the prince on a strip of fine white sand, with his head in the warm sunshine.

Bells now began to ring in a great white temple by the shore and a number of young girls came out into an orchard of orange and lemon trees. When the girls saw the prince they were frightened but soon he revived and they flocked around him. He never looked towards the sea where the little mermaid was resting and she thought he had forgotten her. The most beautiful of the girls led the prince back into the white temple and the little mermaid dived sorrowfully into the water and made her way home.

Many an evening the little mermaid rose from the sea to the inlet where she had left the prince. The fruit in the garden ripened, and the snow melted on the mountain tops, but in all that time she never saw the prince again.

At last she could bear it no longer and she told her sisters about the prince and the coast where she had left him. One of the mermaids knew the country where the prince lived and the following day the mermaids rose from the water in a long line, just in front of the prince's palace: a palace of glistening yellow stone, with great marble staircases. Through clear glass they could see a splendid hall adorned with silk hangings and in its centre lay a large fountain throwing jets of spray towards a sunlit glass dome.

Often in the evenings the little mermaid would swim close to the land and watch the young prince walking in the gardens or sailing his boat. She longed more and more to live with people.

"If men are not drowned," she asked her grandmother one day, "do they live for ever?" "They die too," the old lady answered "and their lives are much shorter than ours. We may live here for three hundred years, but when we cease to exist, we become foam on the water. They have immortal souls which live for ever."

"So I will die and become foam on the sea. Is there nothing I can do to gain an immortal soul?"

"Only if a human being should bestow on you all his love would you then gain an immortal soul."

"I would give my three hundred years to be a human being for one day, and to have a share in the heavenly kingdom," she said sadly.

It was then that the little mermaid decided to visit the sorceress whose abode lay in a grim and desolate part of the sea-bed. As she passed

through a writhing mass of water snakes she was almost choked by slimy weeds of a dank sea forest, and finally she came to a house built of bones. As she swam in the sorceress said: "I know very well why you have come. You want to get rid of your fish's tail, and have two stumps to walk upon so that the young prince may fall in love with you. I will make you a potion and before sunrise you must swim ashore with it. Drink it on the beach; your tail will divide and shrivel up and form into what men call legs. But remember, you can never be a mermaid again and if you do not succeed in winning the prince's love you will only turn into sea foam."

"I will do it," said the mermaid, pale as death.

"But you will have to pay me, too," said the witch. "I will have your voice in return for my precious potion."

"But if you take my voice," said the little mermaid, "what have I left?"

"Why, your beauty, and your eyes full of expression; with these you ought to be able to bewitch a human heart. Have you lost courage?"

"Let it be done then," said the little mermaid.

The witch scoured her cauldron with a bundle of snakes, and piled in the ingredients for the magic brew. As it started to bubble it made strange sounds like crocodiles' weeping. At last the potion was ready. "There it is," said the witch as she cut off the tongue of the little mermaid.

Later that evening, the mermaid rose up through the dark blue water, and saw the moon shine bright and clear over the prince's palace. Slowly she drank the burning, stinging potion and lost consciousness. She awoke to find the handsome young prince fixing his coal black eyes on her. Who was she, he asked, and how did she get there? She looked at him tenderly and with such a sad expression in her eyes that he took her by the hand and led her into the palace. The potion had worked its magic and as she walked she glanced down at her new legs and feet and felt that she was treading on spikes.

In the palace she was clothed in the costliest silks and muslins. All who saw her admired her grace and beauty but the little mermaid was neither able to sing nor speak. Everywhere the prince went she followed and he loved her as one loves a good sweet child.

"Am I not dearer to you than any of the others?" the little mermaid's eyes seemed to say.

He appeared to understand what she was trying to say: "Yes you are the dearest one to me," he told

her, "for you have the best heart of them all. You are like a young girl I once saw but whom I never expect to see again. I was on board a ship which was wrecked and she saved my life. She was the only person I could love in this world."

One day it was announced that the prince was to be married to the beautiful daughter of a neighbouring king, and a splendid ship was fitted out for the journey. "I must go and see the beautiful princess, my parents demand that, but they will never force me to bring her home as my bride; I can never love her."

"You are not frightened of the sea, my beautiful, silent child?" he asked as they stood together on the ship's deck. When the ship entered the harbour of the neighbouring king, church bells rang and trumpets sounded from every lofty tower. There were balls and receptions and when at last the princess made her entrance the little mermaid recognised at once her exquisite beauty.

"It is you who saved me when I lay almost lifeless on the beach," the prince gasped as he saw her.

Their wedding day was set and the little mermaid felt as if her heart would break. As church bells pealed, and heralds rode through the town proclaiming the wedding the little mermaid, dressed in silk and gold, stood holding the bride's train. That same evening the bride and bridegroom went on board ship to the sound of cannons firing and, as darkness grew, colored lamps were hung throughout the ship and sailors danced merrily on deck. The little mermaid knew that soon she would be dead. As she looked overboard she saw her sisters rise from the water, their faces pale as her own, their beautiful long hair no longer floating on the breeze.

"We have given it to the witch to obtain her help, so that you may not die tonight; she has given us a knife, here it is. Plunge it into the prince's heart and you will once more become a mermaid and live out your three hundred years." But when she saw him sleeping peacefully she could not harm him. She kissed his fair brow and threw the knife far out among the waves.

As the sun rose from the sea the little mermaid saw hundreds of ethereal beings floating overhead, their voices so spirit-like no human ear could hear them. Light as bubbles they drifted through the air and suddenly the little mermaid realized that her form had become like theirs.

"You have come to join the daughters of the air!" said one, "a mermaid has no undying soul, her eternal life depends upon an unknown power but by their own good deeds they may create one for themselves. We bring cool breezes to the tropics, we scatter the scent of flowers over the earth, and when, for three hundred years, we have labored to do all the good in our power we gain an undying soul and take part in the everlasting joys of mankind."

On board ship all was again life and bustle, and she watched as the prince with his lovely bride searched for her; they looked sadly at the bubbling foam, as if they knew that she had thrown herself into the waves. Unseen she kissed the bride on her brow, smiled at the prince and rose aloft with other spirits of the air to the rosy clouds which sailed above.

The

Emperor's New Clothes

Once upon a time there lived an Emperor who cared about nothing but his splendid clothes. He had a wardrobe as big as a ballroom, and there he spent all his spare time. He rarely left his wardrobe except to show off his clothes.

The Emperor's wardrobe was famous all over the world, and tailors were always sure of finding a job at the palace – it was considered a great honour to add to his magnificent wardrobe. One day, however, two swindlers came to the Emperor as he was trying on a new suit with purple zig-zags. These swindlers announced that they were weavers, and asked the Emperor if he desired to see proof of their skill. Apparently they could weave the world's most beautiful clothes, with astounding colours and marvellous shifting patterns. Not only that, but a suit of clothes made from their cloth would seem invisible to anyone who was dull or unfit for high office. The Emperor was dumbfounded at the

thought of acquiring clothes that could also become invisible.

"Imagine! With splendid garments like that I could easily discover which of my Councillors are worthy of their office."

The two swindlers were set work at once, and the Emperor left orders that they should be given as many fine materials as they wished. And what materials they demanded! The finest silks and velvets in every colour of the rainbow, along with enough gold and silver thread to sew one hundred suits. All of these materials the swindlers bundled into their own bags while they worked away at the empty looms. The Emperor insisted that no-one should disturb the weavers until they had finished but finally he grew impatient and sent his wisest minister to inspect the work.

As the minister entered the room, he saw the swindlers working hard at their looms. But, as far as he could see, the looms were empty!

"Do come closer," invited one of the swindlers. "Have you come to see how we're getting on?"

"Er. . . yes," stammered the poor minister. "The Emperor himself has sent me."

On hearing this, both swindlers eagerly begged him to give them his honest opinion on the material they were weaving. The minister stared and stared at the looms but he still could see nothing. "Why, I must be unfit for my royal office!" he thought, much astonished. "I must never, ever let the Emperor know, or he will dispense with my services and banish me to the country."

So the minister smiled at the swindlers and assured them that the material was all that could be desired. Then he hurried off to inform the Emperor that the fabulous new suit of clothing was coming on a treat. A few days later the Emperor again became anxious to see how his clothes were getting on; this time he sent one of his most faithful chancellors.

"My goodness gracious me," muttered the chancellor to himself as he entered the room, "these looms are bare!"

He peered through his spectacles at the empty looms then he rushed out of the room, and ran straight to the Emperor to praise the material. "Your majesty *must* make these wonderful men Royal Weavers," he declared.

At this, the Emperor became so curious that he decided to inspect the weavers himself. So, accompanied by several court officials, he marched through the palace, until he reached the weavers' room. He strode forward, impatient to see his new clothes.

But the Emperor himself could not see anything on the looms!

"This is tragic," he moaned to himself. "Whatever shall I do? If I admit in front of all my officials that I can see nothing, I will be the laughing-stock of

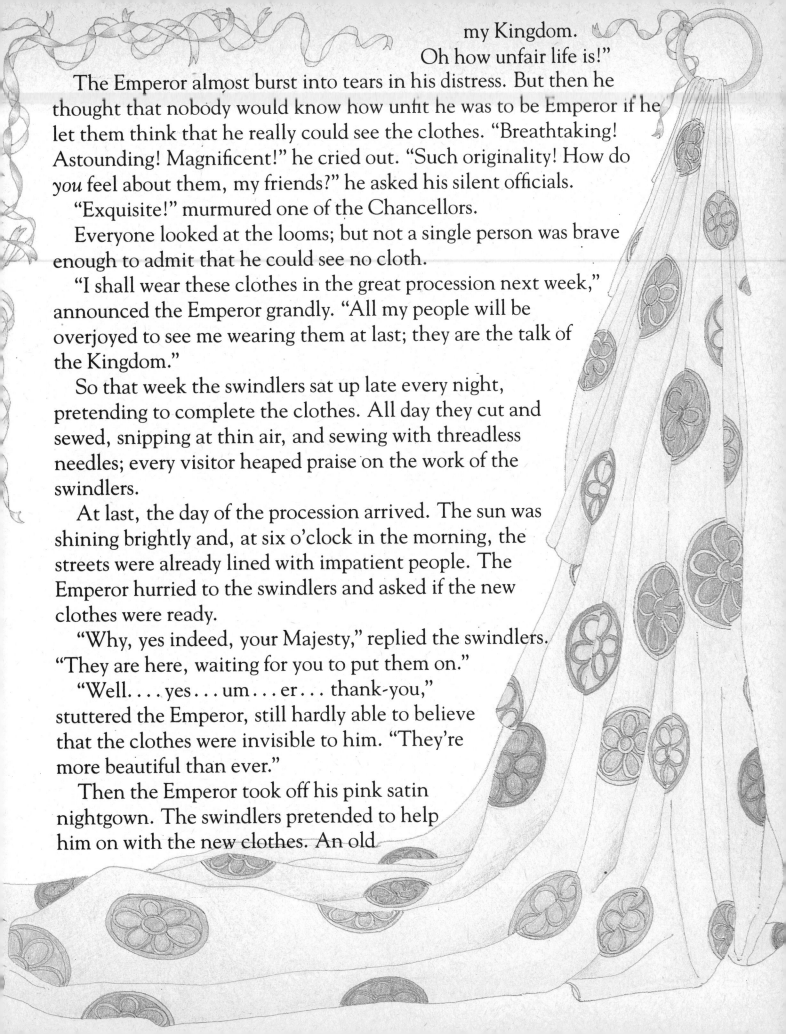

my Kingdom.
Oh how unfair life is!"

The Emperor almost burst into tears in his distress. But then he thought that nobody would know how unfit he was to be Emperor if he let them think that he really could see the clothes. "Breathtaking! Astounding! Magnificent!" he cried out. "Such originality! How do *you* feel about them, my friends?" he asked his silent officials.

"Exquisite!" murmured one of the Chancellors.

Everyone looked at the looms; but not a single person was brave enough to admit that he could see no cloth.

"I shall wear these clothes in the great procession next week," announced the Emperor grandly. "All my people will be overjoyed to see me wearing them at last; they are the talk of the Kingdom."

So that week the swindlers sat up late every night, pretending to complete the clothes. All day they cut and sewed, snipping at thin air, and sewing with threadless needles; every visitor heaped praise on the work of the swindlers.

At last, the day of the procession arrived. The sun was shining brightly and, at six o'clock in the morning, the streets were already lined with impatient people. The Emperor hurried to the swindlers and asked if the new clothes were ready.

"Why, yes indeed, your Majesty," replied the swindlers. "They are here, waiting for you to put them on."

"Well....yes...um...er...thank-you," stuttered the Emperor, still hardly able to believe that the clothes were invisible to him. "They're more beautiful than ever."

Then the Emperor took off his pink satin nightgown. The swindlers pretended to help him on with the new clothes. An old

Councillor stood by, shaking his head in mock amazement and marvelling at the perfect fit. Soon everybody in the room was following his example, shaking their heads like dodos and clucking in astonishment. At last the Emperor was ready. He turned round and round several times in front of the mirror to give the appearance of admiring the clothes. Then the Emperor's most honoured officials pretended to pick up his train.

Crowds were shouting for the Emperor, and all the people were craning their necks and standing on tip-toe in an effort to be the first to see the famous clothes. The Emperor strode into view, and suddenly, after a moment of silence, everyone began cheering and praising the weavers, who were also in the procession. All the people started to admire the non-existent clothes at the top of their voices, for they did not want to look like fools. But one little girl, bored by hearing her parents go on and on about the magnificence of the colours, and the delicacy of the cloth, said loudly: "But he hasn't got anything on!"

"*What* did you say? *He hasn't got anything on?* Why, you silly little girl, of course our Emperor has got something on!" gasped her father.

"Shhhh!" hissed the girl's mother. "The neighbours might hear!"

But the neighbours *had* heard. Gradually the little girl's words were whispered among the crowd until everyone had heard them. Finally all the people cried out together: "*But the Emperor hasn't got anything on!*"

The Emperor heard them clearly, and realised how he had been tricked. Furiously he turned on the swindlers, but they had slipped away.

"There is nothing for it," he thought miserably. "I will simply have to go through with the procession now."

So the Emperor marched on, more upright than ever, and the officials continued to hold up the invisible train.

The Princess and the Pea

Once upon a time, in a far-off kingdom there lived a prince, and he wanted a princess, but then she must be a *real* princess. He travelled right round the world to find one, but there was always something wrong. There were plenty of princesses, short ones, tall ones, fat ones, thin ones, but whether they were real princesses he had great difficulty in discovering. There was always something which was not quite right about them. So at last he returned home again, and he was very sad because he wanted a real princess so badly.

One evening there was a terrible storm; it thundered, with great flashes of lightning, and the rain poured down in torrents. Indeed it was a fearful night.

In the middle of the storm somebody knocked at the palace gate, and the old King himself went to open it.

It was a princess who stood outside, but she was in a terrible state from the rain and the storm. The water streamed out of her hair and her clothes, it ran in at the top of her shoes and out at the heel, but she said that she was a real princess and she had heard that the prince would only marry a real princess and no-one else.

"Well we shall soon see if that is true," thought the old Queen, but she said nothing. She went into the bedroom, took all the bedclothes off and laid a pea on the bedstead; then she took twenty mattresses and piled them on the top of the pea, and then twenty feather beds on the top of the mattresses. This was where the princess was to sleep that night. In the morning they asked her how she had slept.

"Oh terribly badly!" said the Princess. "I have hardly closed my eyes the whole night!

Heaven knows what was in the bed. I seemed to be lying upon some hard thing, and my whole body is black and blue this morning. It is terrible!"

They saw at once that she must be a real princess, after all she had felt the pea through twenty mattresses and twenty feather beds. Nobody but a real princess could have such a delicate skin.

So the prince took her to be his wife, for now he was sure that he had found a real princess, and the pea was put into the Museum, where it may still be seen if no one has stolen it.

Tom Tit Tot

Once upon a time there was a woman and one day she baked five pies. But when they came out of the oven the crusts were rock hard. So she said to her daughter: "Daughter, put those pies on the shelf, and leave them there a little, and they'll be all right."

But the girl said to herself, "Well, what's the use of that. I'll eat them up now." And she set to work and ate them all up.

When evening came the woman said: "Go and get one of those pies. I'm sure the crusts will be soft now." The girl looked and found nothing but the empty dishes. Back she came and said: "No, they are not soft yet."

"Not one of them," said the mother.

"No, not one of them," said the daughter.

"Well, whether they are soft or not," said the mother, "I'll have one for supper."

"But you can't, if they are not soft," protested the girl.

"But I can," said she. "Go and bring the best of them."

"Best or worst," said the girl, "I've eaten them all up, so you can't have any."

Well, the woman was wholly beaten, and she took her spinning wheel to the door to spin, and as she spun she sang:

"My *daughter has eaten five, five pies today,*
My daughter has eaten five, five pies today."

Walking down the street at that very moment was the king himself and when he heard her sing he stopped and said: "What was that you were singing, my good woman?"

The woman was ashamed to let him hear all about her daughter's greed, so she sang instead:

"My *daughter has spun five, five skeins today,*
My daughter has spun five, five skeins today."

"My stars!" said the king, "I've never heard of any one who could do that. Look here, I wish for a wife, and I'll marry your daughter. But," he added, "eleven months out of the year she shall have all she desires but the last month of the year she must spin five skeins every day,

otherwise I shall kill her."

The woman agreed; for she knew what a grand marriage that would be. And as for the five skeins, well, when the time came, they would think of something.

So they were married and the girl had everything she desired. But when the twelfth month drew near, she began to worry about the skeins. But not a word did the king say.

However, on the last day of the eleventh month he took her to a room she had never seen before. "Now, my dear," he said, "you'll be shut in here tomorrow with some food and some flax, and if you haven't spun five skeins by night, off will go your head." And he left her in the room with nothing but a spinning-wheel and a stool.

The girl was terrified and started to cry for she had never even learned how to spin. Suddenly there was a bang and a puff of smoke and the next thing she saw was a small black imp with a long tail walking through the door: "What are you crying for?" it asked.

"Well," she said, "it won't do any harm to tell you, it won't do any good either," and she told the imp all about the pies, and the skeins, and everything.

"Look," said the small black imp, "I shall come to your window every morning, take away the flax, and bring it back spun at night."

"What's your pay?" she asked.

The small black imp looked out of the corner of its eyes, and said: "Three attempts you shall have nightly to guess my name, and if you haven't guessed it before the month is up, you shall be mine."

Well, every day the flax and the food were brought, and every day the small black imp came morning and evening. She never managed to guess its name.

On the last day but one the king came in and said: "Well, my dear, you are progressing so well I've decided to dine here with you tonight."

As they ate their supper he began to laugh.

"What is it?" said she.

"Why," said he, "I was out hunting today, and I got to a place in the wood I had never seen before. I heard a sort of humming in an old chalk-pit, so I got off my horse and took a look. Well, what should be there but the funniest little black imp you ever saw. It had a little spinning-wheel, and was spinning like fury, and twirling its tail. And as it spun, it sang:

"*Nimmy, nimmy not, my name's Tom Tit Tot.*"

When the girl heard this, she could have jumped for joy, but she didn't say a word.

Next day the small black imp looked very full of malice when it came for the flax. "What's my name?" it said.

"Is it Solomon?" said she, pretending to be afraid.

"No it isn't," it said, coming farther into the room.

"Is it Zebedee?" said she.

"No, it isn't," said the imp, laughing and twirling its tail so fast that you could scarcely see it. But now she looked at it and pointing her finger at it, said:

"*Nimmy, nimmy not, your name's Tom Tit Tot.*"

When the imp heard her, it shrieked frightfully, and flew away into the dark, and she never saw it again.

The Ugly Duckling

It was summertime. The wheat was golden, the oats still green, and the hay lay stacked in the rich, low-lying meadows where the stork was marching about on his long red legs. In the sunniest spot stood an old mansion overlooking a deep lake, and great dock leaves stretched from the walls of the house right down to the water's edge; some were so tall that a small child could stand upright under them. Buried in amongst the leaves was a

duck, sitting on her nest of eggs. At last one egg after another began to crack, and the chicks started poking their heads out.

"Quack! quack!" said the mother, "I suppose you are all here now? No! I declare the biggest egg is still there. How long is this going to continue then?" she said as she settled herself back on the nest once more.

Finally the big egg cracked. "Cheep, cheep!" said the young one as he tumbled out.

"Oh, what a monstrous big duckling," exclaimed his mother, "none of the others looked like that."

The day was a gloriously fine one and the sun shone brightly on all the green dock leaves, as mother duck led her new family down to the lake. *Splash!* Into the water she sprang, and one duckling after another plopped in after her. Immediately the water dashed over their heads, but up they came and floated about quite beautifully; even the big ugly grey one swam about with them.

Next she took them into the farmyard where they witnessed a

fearful fight, for two families of ducks were squabbling over the head of an eel. In the end the cat captured it. "That's how things go in this world," said the mother duck, and she licked her bill, for she would have loved to gobble up the eel's head herself.

The other ducks were not happy with the new invasion. "Just look what we have to put up with, as if there were not enough of us about already. Oh dear! look at that ugly duckling," one of them muttered as he flew down and bit him in the neck.

"Let him be," said the mother; "he is doing no harm."

But the poor duckling was made fun of by ducks and hens alike. "He is too big," they all said; and the indignant turkey cock puffed himself up like a vessel in full sail till he became quite red in the face. The poor duckling was at his wits' end, he did not know which way to turn. Every day things grew worse and worse. The duckling was chased and hustled, bitten by the ducks and pecked by the hens. Even his brothers and sisters ill-used him and jeered at him: "If only the cat could get hold of you, you hideous object!"

At last he could stand it no longer. Off he ran straight over the hedge where he so

frightened the little birds they all disappeared. "This is because I am so ugly," thought the poor duckling. On and on he ran until he came to a great marsh where the wild ducks lived. Tired and miserable he stayed there the whole night long without moving. In the morning he hobbled towards a tumbledown little cottage where an old woman lived with her cat and her hen.

"What on earth is that?" said the old woman. Her sight was so bad she mistook him for a large duck. "This is a capital find; now at last I shall have duck's eggs."

The old woman's cat liked to lord it over the duckling and bossed him about whenever she saw fit.

"Do you ever lay eggs?" she asked.

"No," said the duckling quietly.

"Will you have the goodness then to stop all those quacking noises you make!" snapped the cat.

"Can you arch your back, purr, or give off sparks?" asked the cat another time.

"No," said the duckling sadly.

"Then you'd better shut your beak when sensible people are talking."

And so the duckling spent most of his time alone in a corner. One day he found himself longing for the waters of the lake.

He simply had to tell the hen. "What on earth possesses you," she clucked, "haven't you anything else to think about? Lay some eggs or take to purring, and you will soon stop these ridiculous thoughts. You are an idiot; there is no pleasure in having you around."

"I absolutely must go out into the wide world," said the duckling sadly. So back he went to the lakes where every living creature shunned him because of his ugliness.

Autumn came, the leaves in the woods turned brown and red, and the clouds hung heavy with snow and hail. One evening, as the sun was setting in wintry splendour, a flock of large birds appeared; the duckling had never seen anything so beautiful as these dazzling white creatures with their long slender necks. While he was watching, they uttered a peculiar cry, spread out their magnificent wings and flew away from that cold region in the direction of open seas and warmer lands. As they rose high in the sky the ugly little duckling became strangely uneasy. He spun round and round and round in the water like a wheel, craning his neck up into the air in an effort to follow the snow white birds. He did not know what they were, but he felt drawn towards them as he had never before been drawn towards anything else.

Winter was bitterly cold and the duckling was obliged to swim about in the water to stop it from freezing over. Every night the hole in which he swam became smaller and smaller and, in the end, the water froze so hard he found himself stuck fast in the ice.

Early the following morning a farmer rescued the duckling and carried him home. The farmer's children wanted to play with him, but the duckling feared they would ill-use him, and in his fright he knocked over the milk pan. Milk spurted out all over the room. In panic, the duckling flew hither and thither knocking over everything in sight. The farmer's wife screamed, the children chased after him and the duckling flew out of the barn door into the snow-covered bushes.

When spring came the duckling raised his wings and found that they flapped with much greater strength than before. Soon he could fly and one day he landed in a large garden where the apple trees were in full blossom, and the air was scented with lilacs. Just in front of him were three beautiful white swans swimming lightly over the water. At once the duckling recognised the majestic birds he had seen last

autumn: "I will fly to them. They might peck me to pieces because I am so ugly but it won't matter; better to risk being killed by them than to be snapped at by ducks, pecked at by hens, or spurned by every living creature."

So he flew into the water and swam towards the stately swans who darted towards him, their feathers ruffled. As they did so, he looked down into the transparent water and saw his own image reflected, but he could see that he was no longer a clumsy dark grey bird, ugly and ungainly; now he was himself a swan! The big swans greeted him and stroked him with their bills. As they were doing so some little children came to the water's edge and threw corn and pieces of bread into the water. The smallest one cried out: "There is a new one!" And they clapped their hands and danced about and exclaimed that the new one was the prettiest of all; he was so young and handsome.

He felt quite shy and hid his head under his wing; he did not know what to think; he was so happy. He thought of how he had been pursued and scorned, and now they were saying that he was the most beautiful of all. The lilacs bent their boughs into the water before him, and the bright sun was warm and cheering, and he rustled his feathers and raised his slender neck aloft. Never in all his life before had he dreamt of so much happiness.

Chantecleer and Partlet

Once upon a time, in a tiny cottage near a clump of shady trees, there lived a poor widow with her two daughters.

In her yard the widow kept a splendid cock, called Chantecleer. This cock had a most remarkable voice; in all the kingdom Chantecleer had no equal. His voice was merrier than the church organ, louder than the loudest abbey clock, and, indeed, with his crowing he kept time as well as any clock. Not only was Chantecleer blessed with a splendid voice but he was also a most handsome fellow. His feathers shone like burnished gold and his comb, bright orange, was shaped like a crenelated castle wall, and stood up proud and tall. His beak glowed and his feet were of the brightest yellow.

For companionship Chantecleer had seven hens, the fairest of whom was called Partlet.

One morning at daybreak, as Chantecleer was sitting on his perch inside the widow's house, with Partlet at his side and other hens nearby, he started making the most hideous noises, groaning like a man in the middle of a bad dream.

Partlet enquired: "What ever is wrong with you, Chantecleer? Why do you make such a dreadful noise?"

Chantecleer answered: "Please do not take offence, Partlet. I dreamed that I was strutting out in our yard when I saw, among the weeds a hound-like beast who would have killed me stone dead. His coat was not

quite yellow, not quite red, and both his ears and tail were tipped with black. His eye was fierce and fiery and he fixed me with such a look I felt that I would die of fear."

"For shame! What a faint-hearted fellow you are," Partlet burst out. "I cannot love a coward like you. Shame on you!" And so Chantecleer was forced to shrug off his fears and soon he had forgotten all about his terrible dream.

But one day, as Partlet was enjoying a sand bath and Chantecleer was singing to her, he caught sight of a butterfly among the herbs. The butterfly swooped down and, as it did so, Chantecleer saw the fox he had encountered in his dream crouching low among the herbs.

"Cawcaw" cried Chantecleer immediately turning away in terror.

"Where are you going, kind sir," enquired the fox, "surely you are not afraid of me, your friend? I have come on this visit especially to hear you sing. I believe that you have a voice as fine as any angel. Indeed, I have never heard anyone sing better except your own father whose voice was both loud and lordly. Show me, dear fellow, that your voice is the equal of your famous father's".

Chantecleer, delighted to hear such praise from the mouth of the fox, began to

beat his wings. He stood on tiptoe,
stretched up his neck, shut his eyelids
tight and began to crow in a most lordly
fashion. But, after he had sung only a
few notes, the fox seized him by the
throat and ran off towards his den.

Seeing the plight of poor Chantecleer
the hens set up a piteous wail and the
widow and her daughters cried out:
"Help, help. The fox, the fox!" and after
him they all ran, the dog, the cow and
her calf, the pigs, the ducks and geese.
They all chased after the fox and made
such a hubbub, the noise resounded
throughout the woods. As they
approached the fox, Chantecleer just
managed to gasp: "Tell them not to
bother, tell them you are going to eat
me. Tell them to take their noise away."

"Fine!" said the fox, most pleasantly
surprised by Chantecleer's advice, "I'll
do just as you say."

And, as he opened his mouth,
Chantecleer escaped from his jaws and
flew, at once, high up into a tree. When
the fox saw that the cock was free he
pleaded: "Alas, alas, O Chantecleer! So
far as I have given you cause for fear by
seizing you and bearing you away I
have done you wrong, I must admit.
But, sir, I did it with no ill intent.
Come down, and I shall tell you
what I meant."

"No, no," declared Chantecleer.
"You will never again persuade me
to sing and wink my eyes."

Partelet forgave Chantecleer
and never, for the rest of his life,
did Chantecleer listen to flattery.

The Frog Prince

Once upon a time there lived a king who had five beautiful daughters, and the youngest was the most beautiful of all. Close to the king's castle lay a great, dark forest and one day the youngest princess decided to walk amongst the trees. She wandered about for some time until, at last, feeling hot and tired, she sat down by the side of a cool well in the forest glade.

In her hand the princess carried a golden ball, a precious gift from her father, and as she rested by the well she threw up the ball and caught it, then she threw it higher and higher until one time, stretching out her hands to the ball, she let it slip through her fingers. It bounced against a tree, then ricochet off and dropped into the well:

Splash!

The princess peered down into the deep well but

however hard she looked she could not see to the bottom. Tears streamed down her cheeks.

"If only I could get my ball back again, I would give away all my fine clothes and my jewels, and everything that I have in the world," she sighed.

While she was sobbing, and speaking her thoughts out loud a frog popped its head out of the water: "Princess, why on earth are you crying, why do you weep so bitterly?" he asked.

The Princess turned around but when she saw the ugly, squat creature, his face raised to hers, she shuddered in disgust: "Mind your own business. What on earth can you do. If you really want to know, my golden ball has fallen into the well."

The frog answered her, in his deep, kindly voice: "I am not interested in your jewels or in your pearls or in any of your fine clothes. What would I do with them? But, dear princess, if you will only love me and let me live with you, and allow me to eat from your golden plate, and sleep upon your bed, I will fetch your ball."

"What silly things he does say," thought the Princess, "how on earth could anyone love such a grotesque, slimy creature. This well is so deep he will never be able to get out of it."

So she turned to face the frog: "Yes, yes, bring me my ball, please. I will do anything you ask of me, I promise."

Without hesitation, the frog plunged into the well, dropping deep, deep down into the water. After a while he emerged, clutching the golden ball which he let fall at the feet of the princess.

The beautiful golden ball! Eagerly, the princess picked up her toy, overjoyed at seeing it once more. She quite forgot to say good-bye to the frog or to thank him. All her thoughts were directed towards the castle as she started to run through the forest.

"Stay, princess, stay and take me with you. You have given me your word, you

have made me a promise," the frog croaked after her, his voice full of sadness. But the princess was deaf to his pleas and ran faster than ever through the darkening forest.

The following day, just as the princess was sitting at the table with the king and all his court, she heard a strange noise:

Tap, Tap, – Tap, Tap.

It was the sound of tiny feet on the cold marble. Something, some creature, was struggling to climb the marble staircase. The sound continued:

Tap, Tap, – Tap, Tap.

Soon there was a gentle knock at the door and a sad croaky voice called out:

"Open the door, my princess dear,
   Open the door to thy true love here!
   And mind the words that thou and I said
   By the fountain cool in the greenwood shade."

The princess leapt from the table, ran to the door and opened it. There, at her feet, was the quite forgotten frog. She was most terribly frightened. She banged the door shut and returned to the table feeling quite unwell.

"Why do you look so pale, my dear? What has happened?" the King enquired kindly.

"Oh," she answered, trying hard to disguise her feelings, "it is only a slimy frog who just happened to lift my ball out of the water. I sort of made a promise to him that he might live with me here. Truly, I never believed that he would be able to climb out of that deep, slippery well. I wasn't making a *true* promise. Now he is at the door and he wants to come in."

The frog knocked again, most gently, and sounding even more forlorn than before, repeated his request.

"Open the door, my princess dear,
   Open the door to thy true love here!

And mind the words that thou and I said
By the fountain cool in the greenwood shade."

The king listened intently to his words and then turned to the young princess: "As you have made this promise, you must keep it. Go to the door and welcome this kind frog who helped you in your time of need."

The Princess hesitated. She slowly opened the door and the frog hopped quietly into the room and followed her to the table: "Pray lift me upon a chair," he said to the princess, "and allow me to sit next to you." The princess did as he asked and then the frog said: "Put your plate closer to me that I may eat out of it." She pushed her plate towards him and when he had eaten as much as he could, he croaked: "Now I feel so tired; carry me upstairs and put me into your little bed."

And the Princess took him up in her hand and placed him upon the pillow of her own bed where he slept all night long. As soon as it was light, he jumped up, hopped down stairs, and out of the castle. "He is gone at last," thought the princess, "now I shall be troubled no more."

But she was mistaken, for when night came she heard the familiar noise:

Tap, Tap, – Tap, Tap.

Reluctantly, she approached her bedroom door and opened it. The frog hopped in and slept upon her pillow as before.

On the third night the princess was drifting off to sleep when she heard the now familiar sound:

Tap, Tap, – Tap, Tap.

and the frog once more claimed his place on the pillow of the princess. But the following morning she was astonished to find, not the frog squatting on her pillow, but a handsome prince standing at the head of her bed.

The prince's story was a long and sad one. He related to the princess how he had been enchanted by a malicious fairy, who had changed him into the form of a frog, a form in which he was fated to remain until a princess should take him out of the well and let him sleep upon her bed for three nights.

"You," continued the prince, "have broken this cruel charm, and now I have nothing to wish for but to ask you to come with me into my father's kingdom where I will marry you, and love you as long as you live."

The young princess, you may be sure, was not long in giving her consent and as they spoke a splendid carriage drove up with eight beautiful horses decked with plumes of feathers and golden harness. Behind the carriage rode the prince's servant, the faithful Henry, and they all set out, full of joy, for the Prince's kingdom.

After a long journey they reached the end of their destination and there they were married. Much feasting and rejoicing took place and the frog prince and his princess lived happily for the rest of their lives.

A Lion and a Mouse

Once upon a time a lion was walking through the jungle. He was the king of the beasts and all the animals were frightened of him and stood in awe of him. It happened that very day that a small mouse had built his nest directly in the lion's path and the lion stepped on the nest,

squashing the mouse under his
paw. When the lion felt the mouse
wriggling underneath his paw he was angry and thought he
would gobble up the mouse for his supper. But the mouse
asked him if he would kindly spare his life and, because the lion didn't
feel very hungry, he let the mouse go on his way.

Two or three days later, the same lion was lured into a trap, caught in
a hunter's snare. He bellowed for help but none of the beasts of the forest
came near him. However, the same mouse whose life he had spared just
two or three days before, heard the roaring lion and ran to see what was
the matter. When he saw that the lion was trapped, he jumped up on the
lion's back and ran along the rope of the snare. Then he bit his way
through the rope and the lion went free.

And the moral of this story is that if you do a good deed for somebody
that same person will often help when you
yourself are in need of assistance.

Fox and a Crow

One morning a fox was returning to his lair after a night's hunting. He had not caught anything and he was feeling very hungry. As he passed the farmer's house he saw a crow stealing a delicious looking piece of cheese that the farmer's wife had left in the window. His mouth watered and he thought to himself how he could get the crow to give him the cheese. The crow flew off and perched far above his head in a nearby tree. The fox ran to the foot of the tree and started flattering the crow.

"Oh, beautiful bird," said the fox, "so graceful, so delightful and so well loved by everyone. What lovely feathers you have, and how lucky you are to be able to see into the future. Truly you are possessed of all the virtues and I cannot think of any bird so blessed. However, I do not think I have ever heard you sing. If your singing is even half as good as all your other qualities, there cannot be another creature in the whole world so fabulous."

The crow was flattered by this and to show the fox that his voice was as beautiful as the rest of him he opened his beak and started singing so that the fox might hear him. But of course, as he opened his beak the cheese dropped out and the fox snapped it up and ate it in two gulps.

"Ah ha," said the fox, "I spoke of your beauty, but you will notice I said nothing about your brains."

And the moral of this story is beware of flatterers who may just be after something for themselves.

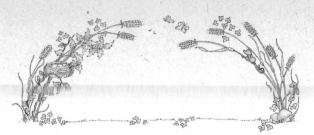

The Bear and the Bees

Once upon a time there was rather a foolish bear who was walking through a wood. It was a very hot day and the bear lay down under a tree and went to sleep. While he was sleeping a bee came and buzzed around his nose. He swatted at the bee with his paw and the bee was so frightened he stung the bear right on his nose.

The bear was furious. He got up, charged into the bee garden and, without stopping to think, he kicked over all the beehives in furious revenge. This made the bees very angry. They flew at the bear and stung him in a thousand places, so that he was forced to run away, wishing that he had never gone near them at all.

And the moral of this story is that it is foolish to try and get revenge for one small injury if by doing so you make hundreds of enemies.

A Peacock
and a Crane

APEACOCK and a crane were talking together in a garden. The peacock was very pleased with his appearance and he spread out his tail to show the crane the full beauty of his feathers.

'My feathers are much finer than yours,' said the peacock. 'Look at the wonderful patterns they make.'

When he heard this boasting the crane sprang into the air and flew round and round above the peacock's head.

'Come and join me,' he taunted. 'It's much more fun flying around in the sky than being stuck on the ground the whole time. Your feathers are all very well but it seems to me they would be better still if they enabled you to fly.'

MORAL: *That which is useful is of more importance than that which is merely ornamental.*

The Hornets
and the Bees

One day some hornets found a piece of honeycomb. They pretended it was theirs, but the bees said: 'No, it's ours'. As they disagreed, they asked a wasp to act as judge for them in this matter. The judge was puzzled, because no one could prove anything. Some longish, brownish buzzing creatures had been seen near the comb, but that did not prove a thing. The trial went on and on for months and months and cost the litigants a lot of money.

At last a wise bee said: 'Enough is enough. We are wasting time, and money and honey is being wasted. Why don't we set to work and make *another* honeycomb, and then the whole world will see that *we* make the honey and not the hornets?'

The bees agreed to this, and soon the wasp judged that it was the bees who won the day.

MORAL: *Disagreements are better settled by common sense than by law and judges who cost a great deal of hard-earned money.*

The Hare
and the Tortoise

ONE day the hare and the tortoise were arguing over who was the best.

'Look at you,' said the hare contemptuously, 'you are dull and heavy and slow. You never get anywhere at all. I am light and gay and graceful. I can run further in a few minutes than you can run in a whole day.'

'That is as may be,' replied the tortoise, 'but I will undertake to run a race with you for a wager.'

'How foolish of you,' said the hare, 'but if you want to be beaten, so be it.'

So they agreed a course and the fox said that he would be the judge. When the day of the race came they started together. The tortoise just kept jogging on at his usual pace and he was soon left far behind and out of sight by the hare, who gambolled along, waving to his friends and stopping to eat certain choice plants by the wayside.

However, the day was hot and after a particularly delicious carrot, the hare decided that he would lie down under a tree and have a short nap.

'After all,' he said to himself, 'I can overtake him in a couple of bounds whenever I please.'

However, the hare slept for longer than he meant. The tortoise plodded on past the hare and came to the winning post first, thereby gaining the prize.

MORAL: *Do not be over-confident: the best person does not necessarily win.*

A Dog and a Cockerel Go on a Journey

A DOG and a cockerel went on a journey together. At nights the dog slept in a hollow tree, while the cockerel roosted in the branches above him. At midnight, the cockerel used to crow 'cock-a-doodle-doo-oo', because that is what he used to do in the farmyard. One night a fox heard him, came to the tree and stood licking his lips at the thought of cockerel for supper. He tried to persuade the cock to come out of the tree: 'What a beautiful voice you have, how well you crow' he said, 'how I wish you would come down so I can shake you by the paw, to show how much I appreciate your fine music.'

'Of course I'll come down,' said the cockerel, 'just tell the door-keeper below to open the door.'

The fox did so, and the dog, who was in the tree, promptly caught him.

MORAL: *Those who try and trick others are often tricked themselves.*

The Eagle
and the Rabbits

ONE DAY an eagle stole some baby rabbits to give to her eaglets to eat. The mother rabbit ran after the eagle, and begged her to have pity on her little ones and save them. But the eagle took no notice, and tore the baby rabbits to pieces. The mother rabbit, in grief and indignation, held a meeting of all the rabbits in her warren, and asked them to help her punish the cruel and savage bird. Now, it is not easy for small and fluffy rabbits to fight a huge and powerful bird like the eagle, but this is what they did. They all went together to the tree in which the eagle lived and nibbled away at the roots until the tree toppled over. All the eaglets fell out and a fox who was waiting below ate them up.

The mother rabbit was comforted by this, to think that although her children were dead, so were those of the eagle.

MORAL: *If many weak people join together, they can often beat one powerful person.*

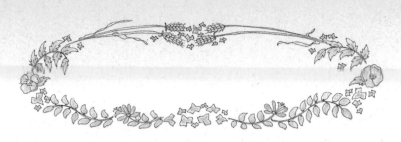

The Fox
and the Grapes

THERE WAS a time when foxes were as fond of
eating grapes as they are of eating lambs, and
it was during this time that a fox who was *very*
fond of grapes, happened to notice a bunch
hanging on a vine. He stood underneath the vine
and licked his lips at the thought of eating such a
delicious treat. Then he tried to get them. He
jumped and jumped and jumped, and tried a
hundred times to get the grapes, but it was no
good: he could not reach them. At last he gave up.

'Oh, bother the grapes,' he said, 'they are sour
anyway.'

And off he went, pretending it did not matter.

MORAL: *It is easy to find an excuse for disappoint-
ment.*

A Wolf
Turned Shepherd

ONCE UPON a time there was a crafty wolf who dressed himself up to look like a shepherd. He had a shepherd's crook, a shepherd's pipe, and he even walked and sat like a shepherd. In fact, he did it so well that once, in the dead of night, he started imitating the shepherd's voice and call as well. But this did not sound so shepherd-like. Indeed, it sounded so odd that the people round about took fright and attacked him, and he was so hampered by all his shepherd's clothes that he could not fight, and he could not escape.

MORAL: *Even the cleverest disguise may be found out.*

A Swallow
and a Spider

A SPIDER who was watching a swallow catch flies decided to make a web to catch swallows. 'Because,' she said, 'I am the one who catches things round here, not the swallow.'

So she spun a swallow-catching web. But the birds, without any difficulty, broke through her web and even flew away with it.

'Well,' said the spider, 'I can see that catching swallows is not one of my talents.'

So she went back to her old trade of catching flies again.

MORAL: *It is wise to learn by experience.*

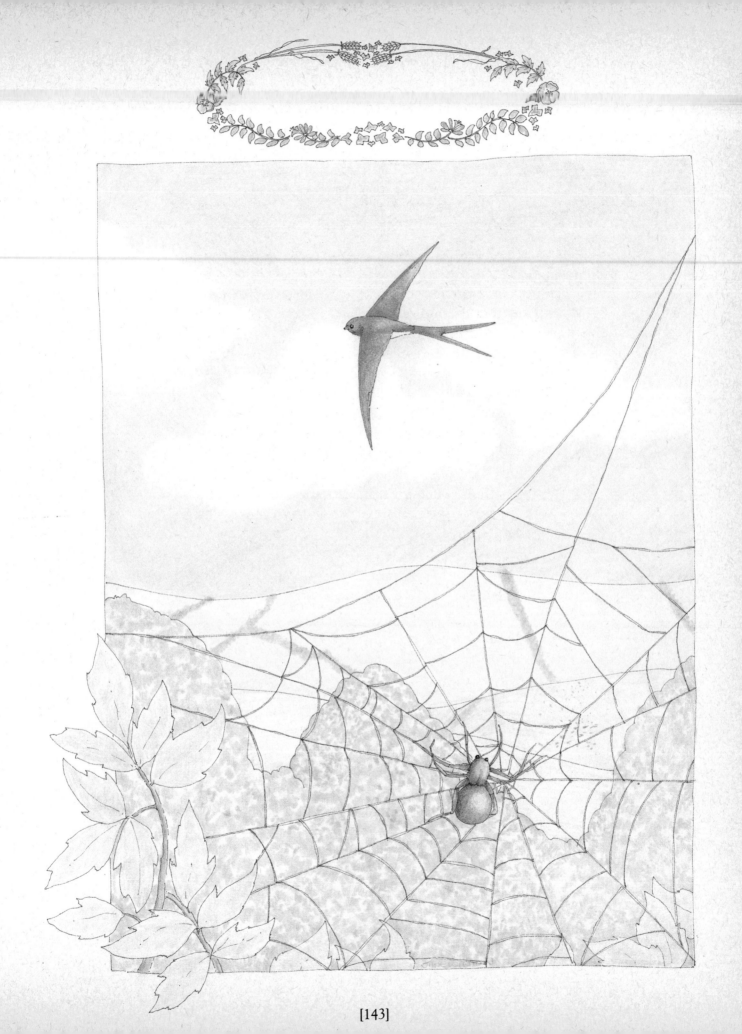

An Oak
and a Willow

AN OAK and a willow tree were arguing about which of them was the strongest, the most reliable, and the most patient. The oak told the willow that the willow was weak and feeble, and let the wind push it about.

The willow said: 'Let us wait until the next storm comes along, and then we shall see who is strongest.'

Very soon after this there was a violent storm, and the wind blew and the rain streamed down. The willow, with its supple branches, blew this way and that, wherever the wind pushed it, and then bounced back, unhurt. But the oak was stiff and stubborn, and refused to bend until a terrible gust came and it broke.

MORAL: *A wise man is prepared to give way so that he can live to fight another day.*

The Thrush and the Jay

'When will you build your nest?' said a thrush to a jay one fine day.

'Oh, by and by,' said the jay. 'It is so nice now that I want to hop and fly and sing while I can.'

'But you can sing while you work,' said the thrush. 'Look, I am gathering moss and twigs to make a nest, and while I work, I sing too. Listen.'

And she sang a fine song.

'Well,' said the jay, 'if you want to slave your life away, that is fine by me.' 'Well,' thought the thrush, 'if you *don't* build your nest it won't be fine for you.' But she said nothing, and the two birds proceeded to occupy themselves, each in her own way. The thrush hatched out five baby thrushes, and fed and sheltered them. The jay thought this dull work, but finally she threw a few sticks together, higgledy-piggledy, to make a nest, and laid her eggs in it, even though the nest was half finished.

One night there was a storm. The wind blew the jay's nest about and all her eggs fell out and broke on the ground. The jay was heartbroken, but the thrush and her little ones were safe and sound and had plenty of time to work, rest and play.

MORAL: *There is a proper time to work and a proper time to play.*

JANE HARVEY·WINTON

The Crab
and its Mother

A MOTHER crab said to her child: 'Don't walk sideways, dear, and don't drag your claws crossways over the wet rocks.'

'Mother,' said the baby crab, 'If you were to walk straight yourself, then I could walk behind and copy you.'

MORAL: *It is better to teach by example than by command*.

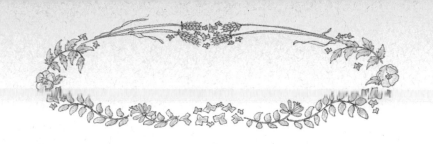

A Mountain and a Mouse

THERE WAS once a people who lived at the foot of a huge mountain. One day the mountain made a terrible noise, thundering and roaring, and the people were afraid, wondering what terrible monster was about to emerge. When at last the mountain opened to reveal the cause of all the roaring, there appeared not a terrible monster, as they had feared, but a tiny, ridiculous mouse.

MORAL: *An awful fuss is often made about nothing*

An Eagle
and other Birds

SOME BIRDS were boasting among themselves: the hawk prided herself on her mighty wings; the crow, on her ability to see into the future; the nightingale boasted of her delicate singing; the peacock, of its beauty; the partridge, on its neatness; the wren, on its brave spirit; the duck, on its paddling, and the heron, on its supposed ability to prophesy the weather.

The eagle listened to all these boasts and said: 'This is all very well, but I have a sharp eye – let me carry one of you into the sky and I shall demonstrate my superiority.'

So the wren climbed onto the eagle, and the eagle soared into the sky and said: 'Can you tell what that speck is below?' The wren said she could not. 'It is a black sheep without a tail,' said the eagle, 'watch while I swoop to get it and eat it.'

And the eagle swooped, and fell straight into a trap.

'There,' said the wren, 'if only you had been as quick to spot the danger as you were to spot the sheep, you would have noticed the man setting up his trap near the sheep.'

MORAL: *Even the sharpest person may be caught in a trap.*

A Swallow
and Other Birds

A FARMER was sowing flax. A swallow – which is a bird well known for its sense and foresight – called all the little birds together and said: 'Look what the farmer is doing. He is sowing flax, and flax is what traps and nets to snare us are made of. Go behind the farmer and pick up the seeds before they can start growing.'

But the birds took no notice, and the seeds took root and started to grow. Once again the swallows warned the birds of the dangers of flax, and told them it was still not too late to stop the damage. But once again, they took no notice, so the swallow said goodbye to her friends in the woods and went to live in the city. In due course the flax was harvested and woven into rope to make nets with. And the nets caught the birds – those very same birds whom the swallow had warned. The birds then realised how stupid they had been not to listen to the swallow, but it was too late: they were caught.

MORAL: *Fools will not believe in the effects of causes until it is too late to prevent them.*

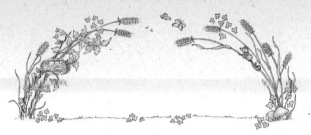

A Jackdaw
Borrows some Feathers

A JACKDAW wished to appear very grand, so he stole or borrowed all the fine feathers he could find and dressed himself up in them. And then he said: 'I am the grandest bird in the whole sky.' He was so puffed up with pride that his friends became jealous of him, and started to pluck out his borrowed feathers. And when every bird had plucked out a feather, the silly jackdaw had nothing left and sat there naked.

MORAL: *It is foolish to take pride in borrowed finery.*

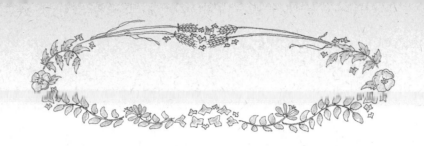

Two Donkeys

TWO DONKEYS were crossing the river. One was carrying salt, the other was carrying sponges. The donkey carrying the salt staggered under the weight of his burden, and fell into the water, but the water dissolved the salt so he soon got up again and went on his way feeling much better.

When the donkey carrying sponges saw how much more cheerful his companion appeared to be for the fall, he decided to follow his example, and he lay down in the river. But the water which had dissolved the salt sank into the sponges and made them forty times heavier, and the poor donkey drowned under their weight.

MORAL: *What is good in one case may be bad in another.*

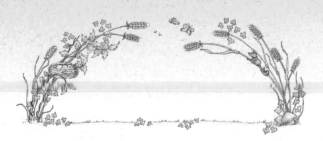

The Cat and the Mouse

ONE DAY a mouse saw a piece of bacon, and, while trying to get it, fell into the trap. A cat who was passing by saw the bacon and the prisoner and set about getting them both.

'Mouse,' he said, in a gentle wheedling voice, 'we have been enemies for so long that I am sick of it: let's be friends in future, do you agree? If so, I can help you.'

The mouse agreed most warmly to this. So the cat suggested that, as proof of their new friendship, the mouse should open the trap door so they could shake hands.

'By all means,' said the mouse. 'All you have to do is lift up that board by pulling down the long piece of wood which sticks out of it.'

The cat did so, and by doing so, opened the trap. The mouse scampered away into her hole with the bacon. The cat followed, but was too late: 'Well,' he said to comfort himself 'it doesn't really matter. The bacon was old and the mouse was very thin.'

MORAL: *Those who try and cheat often find they have been outwitted.*

[160]

An Ant
and a Pigeon

A<small>N ANT</small> was drinking at the side of a stream. Suddenly, she fell in. A wood pigeon who was flying past took pity on her, and threw her a little branch to catch hold of. The ant climbed on to the branch and so was saved from drowning. Soon after this, the ant noticed a man aiming a gun at the pigeon. Immediately she ran up to the man and stung him, so that he did not fire straight, and the pigeon flew away unhurt.

MORAL: *If you do a kind act, you may find yourself unexpectedly rewarded.*

The
Discontented Dog

A DOG saw a cat on top of a wall and said: 'I wish I could get up there. It must be nice to be so high. But I can't climb.'

And he was cross, and would not wag his tail. Then he came to a pond and said: 'How I wish I could live in a pond all day. Then I wouldn't be so hot.'

And he shut his eyes and lay down on the grass, while the fish in the pond wished they too could lie in the fresh green grass.

Soon he got up and went back along the road, and as he went he heard a bird say: 'I wish I could play all day long like that dog, and have a house made for me to live in. I have to fly to and fro all day, and my wings get so tired.'

And then, when he got back to the high wall, he heard the cat say: 'There goes that spoilt old dog, going home for his dinner. How I wish I was given meat as he is. I have had no food all day. How I wish I was like that dog.'

MORAL: *It is foolish to envy others, forgetting your own advantages.*

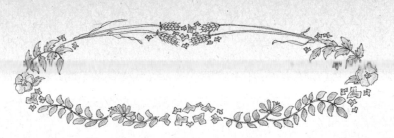

The Eagle,
the Cat and the Pig

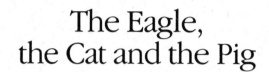

AN EAGLE, a cat, and a pig lived in a tree together. The eagle nested at the top of the tree, the cat lived in the hollow trunk, and the pig lived at the bottom.

Now the cat was a troublemaker, and went telling tales to the eagle: 'You had better watch out,' she said, 'because the pig is always grubbing about at the bottom of the tree and one day she'll make it fall down, *then* where shall we be?'

And then, not content with that, she went to the pig and said: 'Just think what danger you are in. There's an eagle at the top of this tree and she is constantly watching your piglings, in the hopes of being able to eat them for her supper.'

The cat then went back to her kittens and guarded them by day and crept out at night to find food for her family. But the eagle did not dare move from her nest, for fear of the pig, and the pig did not dare leave her piglings for fear of the eagle. And so they both kept guard until they starved for lack of food, and left their children to the cat to take care of.

MORAL: *If you listen to tale-tellers, you will have no peace.*

The Ant and the Cricket

A SILLY young cricket sang all through the warm summer months, but when winter came he began to complain: 'My cupboard is empty,' he said 'and there's no food to be found – what shall I do?'

At last, he was so cold and hungry and wet he set off to ask a hardworking ant if he could borrow a little food, and a corner of his shelter.

'I will pay it back very soon,' he said, 'but if you don't help, I shall die.'

'I have every sympathy with you,' said the ant, 'but we ants never borrow and we never lend either – it is our rule. Tell me, didn't you store up food and shelter when the weather was warm?'

'No,' said the cricket, 'I did not. It was so warm and jolly that I sang all day and all night, and all nature rejoiced with me.'

'Did you say you *sang*?' said the ant, 'then why don't you try dancing now?'

MORAL: *If you don't work when you should you must expect to suffer the consequences.*

The Dog in the Manger

A CHURLISH, envious dog got into a manger, and lay there growling and snarling so that the horses could not eat the hay and oats which the farmer provided for them. The dog, of course, could not eat the hay himself, but he was so mean and nasty he preferred to risk starving himself rather than let anyone else benefit from the food he could not eat.

MORAL: *It is churlish and mean to stop other people using things which we cannot use ourselves.*